ARCH

A One Love Short Story

NATIONAL BESTSELLING AUTHOR

Deborah Fletcher Mello

MaGREGOR PRESS

Published by MaGregor Press

ISBN-10: 0-9979481-4-0
ISBN-13: 978-0-9979481-4-1

ARCH

Printed in the United States of America
First printing, October 2017

This is dedicated to all the girls
who have ever had a dream!
Let nothing deter you.
Continue to DREAM BIG!
Because everything is possible! #iamagem

And especially to Kendra D. Holiday! Your son's
movie star name inspired one hell of a hero!

ACKNOWLEDGMENTS

As always, I must first give thanks to God for His many blessings, for only through Him are all things possible.

I am honored to have one of the greatest street teams who support, encourage, and keep me on my toes. Deborah's Diamonds are a band of warrior women with the biggest hearts and spirits who give selflessly of themselves each, and every day, to promote my books and support my endeavors. I have been enriched by their presence in my life and the bonds of sisterhood that have been formed between us is magnanimous!

Diamonds are rare, multifaceted, precious jewels. They are the ultimate gemstone having few weaknesses and many strengths. They are as beautiful in their natural state as they are when polished. They are tough as nails, individually unique, and exquisitely beautiful.

Deborah's Diamonds are all these things and so much more! I joyously celebrate each of them and every exceptional quality they bring to our amazing literary family. They are invaluable to me and I am grateful to be blessed with their friendship. Hugs and kisses to Nanette Kelley, Toni Bonita Robinson, Louise Brown, Jennifer Copeland, Kay Edmondson, Jackie Williams Ferriere, Tracy Hale, LaVern W. Perschell, and Reshemah Wright.

And lastly, gratitude and well wishes to former Diamond Cynthia Taylor. May your blessings be many, now and always.

ONE

Thirty-two-year-old Archer Santana owned some twenty-thousand square feet of the most exquisite ocean front real estate in Cambria, California and despite having circled the numerous rooms multiple times, the young woman was feeling claustrophobic. It didn't make sense, but not much did anymore.

Finding her way back to the oversized family room she stood staring out to the panoramic views of sand and water that sat beyond the confines of the glass wall. The landscape outside was calm and serene against the threads of a grey-blue sky. The glass and stone home sat perched on the edge of a cliff, nothing but sand, rocks, and water beneath. White-capped waves crashed against the shore and with each spray of water that shot into the cool evening air, Archer felt as if a prayer was being shot straight to heaven. With the first rays of the new day sun trying to find its place amongst the clouds above, the vista was absolutely breathtaking.

There was a time when her home and its location would have given her great comfort, but not this time. Archer was feeling anxious. She imagined that her name was being headlined in every media outlet and news report around the nation, castigating her reputation. Fans were probably weeping for her; strangers gossiping about the tragedy that had suddenly become her life.

Since rising out of her bed that morning it had quickly becoming just another day of discontent and unhappiness. Archer was done with it all, determined to change her fate by any means necessary.

The coveted fame and notoriety she'd garnered no longer meant anything. The riches and excesses were useless. Archer had reached a point of no return and in her mind, she had a host of people to thank, beginning with her mother and ending with her soon-to-be ex-husband.

Moving across the room to the large mahogany bar she flipped through the stack of tabloid magazines that had been left on her doorstep. Front and center, film heartthrob Paulo Santana headlined each one, news of his many indiscretions spreading like wild fire. Archer tossed them all to the floor, disgust fueling nothing but anger and frustration. Paulo had hammered the final nail into her soul. He had snatched the rug from beneath her and had left her broken. Now it was time to show all of them her appreciation and make them regret every, single thing they had ever done to hurt her heart.

Not even the most persistent paparazzi would see what was coming, she thought as she washed a handful of sleeping pills down with a large glass of red wine. She took a deep breath as she swallowed once and then again, struggling not to gag the mixture back up. As far as she was concerned, she thought, Archer Santana was about to take her life back and to hell with everyone who tried to stand in her way.

On the red eye from New York City to Los Angeles, Sinclair Cooper jotted down production notes for the documentary that he was producing on the infamous songstress Archer Santana. A renowned filmmaker and photojournalist, Sinclair was best known for his award-winning documentaries and photographic storytelling. Telling Archer Santana's story had become his latest obsession and he was only just beginning to scratch the surface to get to the tales that had never been told to the public before.

With the pilot announcing their impending landing, he returned his seat and tray to an upright position. Sinclair heaved a deep sigh. Thoughts of Archer Hall Santana were lingering in his head like a virus, slow growing but lethal if not checked.

Archer. Arch to her closest friends and family. There had been something about the woman that haunted him. Maybe it was the air of vulnerability that she exuded when she tried so desperately not to. Maybe it was the hint of wanting that seemed to linger in her gaze when he'd met her stare with one of his own, the moment leaving them both speechless.

His agent, and brother-in-law, Roman Wright, who also happened to be Archer's agent, had been pleading with him for months to consider doing a profile piece on Archer. Roman had promised him unlimited access to the star, assuring him that she would be totally open to the process and completely honest and forthcoming.

But Sinclair had resisted. Flashing a spotlight on the renowned diva was out of sync with the social commentary he preferred to espouse. He hadn't known what had possessed him to approach her as Archer sauntered to the end of the red carpet at the Grammy Awards. The designer gown she'd worn had fit her curvaceous body like a glove, hugging each dip and crevice like paint to a wall. She'd been stunning!

Her dark eyes had been haunting, seeming to stare deep into his core and out of the blue he was introducing himself, asking if she was still interested in having him interview her for a documentary about her life. With a tenacity that was true to his character he had promised to tell her story like it had never been told before.

Archer had eyed him from head to toe and back again, saying nothing as she took the business card he'd been extending in her direction. She'd gestured ever so slightly with her head, eyeing him a second time, and then she'd smiled, the sweetness of it sending a shiver down the length of his spine. Before she could answer, her security team had hemmed him up against a wall as if he were a threat to national security and it was necessary to usher her out of harm's way.

A week later, as news of her husband Paulo Santana's flagrant infidelity torpedoed through the media, including rumors of a tryst with the superstar's mother, Archer had called him. She'd called, wanting to know if he intended to sensationalize her story like all the other journalists or if he was really interested in telling the truth. The absolute truth, *every dirty ounce of it*, had been her exact words. When he'd said yes, so had she. And now he was landing in California, anxious to discover what made Archer Santana tick.

It had begun to rain, a fine mist of moisture spraying from the sky. After picking up his Escalade from the long-term parking deck, Sinclair exited the airport parking lot and headed west toward Cabrillo Highway. He was anxious to see Archer again, the emotion bordering on high school exuberance and he had no explanation for it.

Taking two deep breaths to calm the wave of nervous energy he couldn't help but wonder what life was like for the young woman. How could she have found any normalcy in her day-to-day existence when everything about the lifestyle she'd been raised in had been anything but normal? After an hour with Archer's mother it had become clear that Archer's childhood had been stolen from her even before her birth. She'd been dealt a heavy hand of dysfunction, the cards clearly not in the girl's favor.

Pulling into the circular drive that led to her oceanfront home, Sinclair was instantly overwhelmed by the view. Exiting the vehicle, he took a deep inhale of salted air, savoring the cool rush of morning mist into his lungs. An outdoorsman, he loved everything about the natural setting, sensing that Archer did also, or she would not have invested in such a property. He was even more anxious to discover what moved Archer Santana's spirit.

Reaching into the backseat he pulled a cellophane bag of pink cotton candy into his hands, a gift he hoped would break the ice between them. Her mother had told him it was her favorite.

Moving to the front entrance he rang the doorbell. Minutes later no one had answered the door. Sinclair glanced down at his wrist watch. He was actually a few minutes early for his appointment. He couldn't imagine Archer leaving before he'd even arrived. From everything he'd learned about her, she was not only prudent, but always professional and meticulous about being on time. He drew his cell phone to his ear, pushing the redial button for his last call. Within seconds the phone was ringing inside the spacious home and there was still no answer.

Glancing around the immaculately landscaped property, Sinclair peeked through the glass front for any sign of movement. Easing around the side of the house he peered into a side window, but saw no one. He heaved a deep sigh, annoyance creasing his forehead as he speculated where Archer could possibly be.

Moving to the back of the house he took in the décor of the rear patio, stepping casually around a cushioned lounge chair that meshed nicely with the outdoor space. The rear blinds were wide open, welcoming the morning view. It afforded him the opportunity to peer right into her lavish home.

Pressing his face to the glass he peeked inside. The sliding glass door led into a large family room. The room was in total disarray, looking like a hurricane had blown through it. Furniture was tossed about, paper and clothes scattered everywhere, and then he saw her, her limp body slumped sideways on the sofa. Nervous tension tightened every muscle as he knocked anxiously, hoping that he was only pulling her from a deep slumber.

When she didn't move to answer, he stifled the urge to panic. Reaching for the door handle, he fought against the lock, the panel of glass refusing to budge. With no other recourse, Sinclair grabbed one of the wrought iron chairs and slammed it against the plate of glass, shards shattering to the floor inside and the ground outside of the spacious home.

Rushing inside, Sinclair moved quickly to Archer's side, dropping everything in his hands to the glass topped table. He pressed two fingers against the carotid artery in her neck. There was a strong pulse and he heaved a sigh of relief as he took in the remnants of drugs and drink strewn across the table top.

Gently slapping her face, Sinclair called her name. "Archer? Wake up. You have to wake up, Archer!" he said as he reached to make her stand, pulling her to her feet as he supported what little weight her lithe frame possessed. "You have to wake up and walk for me, Archer," he said loudly. "Archer!"

Archer eyes opened, fluttering wildly as she fought to focus. "Wha...what?" she said, her voice barely a whisper. "Leave...leave me alone," she whined. "I want...want...I just want to sleep."

"Maybe later," Sinclair responded. "But not right now," he said firmly, dragging her across the room. "Now walk!"

Archer's body tightened in defiance, anger rippling through her spirit. As she began to struggle, Sinclair tightened the grip he had around her torso, refusing to let her go.

"That's right, baby. You fight," he chimed as he forced her to walk from one end of the room to the other and back.

The sound of Sinclair's voice broke through the fog that clouded Archer's head. *Who was he calling baby?* This wasn't the dream she'd been hoping for. Nor was it the rest she desperately needed. *Why was this man disturbing her sleep? And who the hell was going to pay for her glass door?* Then she saw the cotton candy he'd dropped against the tabletop.

"I wasn't trying to kill myself," Archer hissed between clenched teeth. She took a second sip of the hot coffee Sinclair had made for her.

She watched as he twisted the pill bottle around in his hand, pausing to read the prescription label and twisting the container over again.

"I wasn't!" she snapped a second time. "I just needed to get some sleep!"

"The label says you were only to take two pills and not with alcohol."

She blinked forest thick lashes as she narrowed her gaze on the man. Clearly, he had to know it had all been a horrible mistake. She blew a heavy sigh.

"Why are you here again?" Archer questioned, her brow creased as she struggled to think, her memory seeming to fail her.

"I'm here to pick you up. We're filming you this week for your documentary."

Recall was swift, everything coming into focus with the third and fourth sip of her coffee.

Archer stood abruptly. "You're paying for that window," she quipped, inhaling the salt air blowing through the opening.

Sinclair chuckled. "It's already being handled. By the time we get back it will be fixed like new."

"It better be," she said. Archer turned, then paused, spinning back around. She studied him momentarily, her gaze sweeping from head to toe as he eyed her just as intently. Sinclair Cooper was a beautiful man, tall, dark and handsome to the nth degree. He was Hershey's chocolate dark with a meticulously trimmed beard and mustache against skin that was marble smooth. He seemed quiet and unassuming, yet his presence commanded your full and undivided attention.

"Thank you for not calling the police," she said. "The press would have had a field day if they found out."

He nodded. "I'm still not sure I did the right thing," he answered. "You'll have to convince me you don't have a problem that's doomed to repeat itself."

"I said it was an accident."

"And I'm saying, I don't know if I believe you."

They stared, continuing to assess each other. The moment was intense and consuming, no one having ever challenged Archer before. She didn't bother to respond. She turned instead and moved past him to the table and the cotton-candy that rested where he'd left it. Picking up the bag, she tore open the cellophane container and pulled a piece of the sweet confection between her fingers.

"Really," she reiterated as she swept past him again, headed in the opposite direction. "I really wasn't trying to hurt myself."

TWO

"Cotton candy! That child never wanted to eat anything but cotton candy!" the woman cackled, her mind skating over the memories. "And always before a concert!"

Sinclair Cooper shifted in his seat, jotting a note down in the ringed binder that rested in his lap. He smiled politely, and Alana Hall smiled back.

"But that's not what you want me to talk about, is it, Mr. Cooper?" the woman questioned, her dark eyes meeting his.

"It's fine, ma'am. I want you to…"

She interrupted him. "Please, don't call me ma'am. I'm not that old," she said tossing the length of her sable hair over her shoulder. She cringed, her nose wrinkling with displeasure.

Sinclair eyed the woman curiously. Alana Hall wasn't old, his research showing that she had just celebrated her fifty-sixth birthday. But her too fast lifestyle had not served her well. She was no longer the glowing beauty men had lusted after in the nineties, watching her sing and dance in her music videos. Years of some seriously bad habits had ruined her complexion, painted dark rings around her eyes and had left her with a persistent cough that sounded as if she were ready to hack up a lung. Even then a cigarette dangled between her stained fingers and her hands shook as if she were epileptic.

Her face was heavily caked with makeup, false eyelashes looking like large bugs taped to her eyes. Garish red lipstick painted her mouth and too light foundation made her seem ghostly. Her clothes were ill-fitting, two sizes too small for the wealth of weight that had plumped her petite frame. But she still carried herself with the same royal air that had been the trademark of her career. She'd been known as Alana Hall, Queen of Song, right up until the day her only daughter had dethroned her.

Sinclair smiled again. "I want you to share anything you desire about your daughter. So please, tell me about the cotton candy."

Alana met his curious gaze for a brief moment and then she rose from her seat, moving to stand and stare out the window as she drifted into the memories.

The child had only wanted cotton candy, she thought, as the young girl massaged the bruise that was rising across her right cheek. She couldn't begin to reason why she'd slapped her face for asking, just that the persistent question had become an annoying whine. So, Alana Hall had backhanded her daughter as if the child were far older than her eight years.

Archer met her mother's intense glare. The harsh look dared the little girl to question her authority. Archer glared back, her eyes misting ever so slightly, but she refused to cry. Alana was just too through with the child's attitude and she said so.

"Why do you have to annoy me, Archer? You get everything you want and all you do is beg and whine for more. You are driving me crazy!" the woman screamed, oblivious to the nanny who'd come rushing in to intervene.

Frances Mink cleared her throat, her hands clasped tightly together in front of her. "Ms. Hall, is there something I can give you and Archer a hand with?" The woman was smiling sweetly in Archer's direction, her soothing tone intent on calming the beast that was Archer's mother.

Alana took a deep breath, inhaling once, and then again, before speaking. "Get Archer some damn cotton candy," she commanded, pushing the length of her hair behind both ears. "I go on stage in thirty minutes and her goddamn whining is getting on my last nerve."

The older woman nodded politely. "Of course," she said, extending her hand toward Archer. "Come on, baby girl. Come with, Minky. Let's go find you some cotton candy."

Archer hurried to Frances' side, clutching at the sturdy fingers that tightly wrapped around her own. She cut her eye in her mother's direction, her gaze narrowing into tight slits as she tossed the woman a harsh look over her small shoulders.

"I hate you," Archer said, her even tone disconcerting. "I hate you and you look like a big, fat cow in that ugly dress," she hissed.

Alana pursed her lips tightly together, her hands dropping to the slight bulge of flesh that girdled her abdomen. She ran her hands down the short length of designer gown draped around her thick body. "I hate you more, you little bitch!" Alana snarled back as she suddenly ripped at the beaded fabric until it was scattered across the floor. "And you better not screw up tonight!"

As Frances hurried Archer out of the room, pushing the little girl ahead of her, she gestured for Alana's personal stylist. The two women both rolled their eyes skyward as the stylist scurried to Alana's side with a new dress in hand. As the door slammed harshly behind them, Archer smiled brightly, deeply satisfied as she skipped eagerly down the length of hallway.

Two and a half hours later, at the end of her mother's musical set, Archer stood in the wings of the massive coliseum waiting for the introduction that would bring her out onto the stage. Frances had wiped the last traces of crystallized sugar from her mouth and hands and had slipped her into a white lace shift that was a replica of the one her mother was wearing. The stylist had twisted her long curls into an updo and had done her makeup so that there was no mistaking whose child she was.

Archer looked down to the patent-leather shoes with the slightest of heels that adorned her feet. She loved new shoes. One day she would have as many pair as she wanted. No one, most especially her mother, would be able to tell her no. Because one day everybody would be paying to hear her sing, fans would be flocking to her concerts, and she would be the best-selling artist of all times, exceeding anything her mother had even imagined accomplishing.

Frances knelt to meet the child at her eye level. "Are you ready, Arch? Ready to knock 'em dead?"

Archer grinned as she nodded her head. She was always ready to sing. Singing was as necessary as breathing as far as Archer was concerned.

Frances winked an eye at her. "Good girl," she said, reaching for a bottle of organic honey and a teaspoon. She poured the sweet substance into the small ladle and passed it to Archer who swallowed it eagerly. Archer then reached for two large wedges of lemon and sucked the fruit from the rind, the honey masking the sour with sweet.

Behind them the music transitioned, ending Alana's song and cueing up Archer's introduction. Frances winked a second time, wrapping the little girl in a warm hug. "Break a leg," she whispered into Archer's ear.

Out on the stage Alana was in full performance-mode. "Thank you, thank you," she chimed, applause ringing through the air. A spotlight was shining down on her. "This is my favorite part of the show," the woman said, smiling brightly as she worked the stage. "I don't often get to sing with such talent, so it makes me very happy to sing with the young lady I want to introduce to you all! Ladies and gentlemen, if you would please, put your hands together for my precious daughter, Archer!"

At the sound of her name Archer grabbed the microphone being extended in her direction and skipped out onto the stage. As another spotlight followed her to her mother's side and the audience came to their feet to applaud, Archer grinned brightly, waving her small hand in greeting. Alana leaned to wrap her arms around Archer's torso, and Archer went through the pretense of hugging her mother back.

The crowd was still cheering and applauding as Alana took a single step backwards, gesturing toward her daughter with an open palm. "The magnificent Archer Hall, ladies and gentlemen!"

"Hello, Chicago!" Archer chimed into her microphone.

Alana tossed her head back in a hearty laugh. "So, what are you going to sing for us tonight?" she asked as if she didn't know.

"I'd like to sing an old classic," Archer nodded. "A throwback to the Beatles!"

Alana laughed again. "What do you know about the Beatles?" she asked, raising her eyebrows toward the audience. "You're too young to know the Beatles!"

"I know good music," Archer grinned, winking her own eye at the crowd.

Alana purred. "That's my baby!" she said. She focused her gaze back on Archer. "And what Beatles classic do we get to hear?"

"I'm going to sing *Blackbird*," Archer responded.

Her mother nodded, clapping her hands together as she stepped out of the spotlight. "Well, let me get out of the way so you can do your thing, darling!"

Standing front and center, Archer closed her eyes tightly, tilting her head ever so slightly as an acoustic guitarist eased on stage behind her, the man's hands skating easily over his guitar strings. An accompanying drum beat added a sultry, seductive mood to the moment that rivaled the Dionne Farris version of the song. Then Archer opened her mouth and sang.

"Blackbird singing in the dead of night...Take these broken wings and learn to fly...All your life, you were only waiting for this moment to arise..."

The little girl was petite in stature but the booming voice that suddenly erupted from her small frame was in a league of its own. A low hush fell over the audience, the crowd shifting forward in their seats as if they might miss a note. Her tone was strong and confident, belying her eight short years and the drama that had been her life just minutes earlier.

Archer opened her wide eyes, looking out over the crowd. *"Black bird singing in the dead of night...Take these sunken eyes and learn to see, all your life, you were only waiting for this moment to be free..."*

Off stage Alana could have cared less about her daughter's stellar performance. Alana would have locked the kid away at boarding school if she'd had the opportunity, but her agent, manager, publicist, and record company had seen the goldmine that was Archer the first time the kid had bum rushed her mother on stage to sing with her a year earlier.

After much coercion and the threat of cancelling her contracts, Alana had agreed to write Archer into the show. The decision had skyrocketed her public approval rating, her adoring maternal image overshadowing all the other crap being written in the tabloids about her. In public, Alana gave them all what they wanted. In private, Alana gave her young daughter next to nothing and Archer didn't want a thing from her either.

Alana heaved a deep sigh as she popped two pills into her mouth and chased them both with a swig of vodka from a pocket-sized decanter.

Clasping the silver cross that dangled from the length of chain around her neck, she pulled the stem from its top and sniffed a line of cocaine from the slim spoon then screwed the unit back together. As the effect of the drug began to kick in, she stepped out on stage to join her only child in the chorus.

Clasping Archer's hand in her own, Alana sung with her, the two looking at each other adoringly. *"Blackbird fly, Blackbird fly... Into the light of the dark black night...You were only waiting for this moment to arise..."*

As the song came to an end, mother and daughter hugged and the crowd roared their approval, the applause thunderous as the audience came to their feet. And then the curtain dropped, hiding them from public view.

Archer turned to look up at her mother, her expression emotionless. "I want to sing two songs from now on or I'm going to tell everyone how you beat me," she pronounced, her intent clear as she pointed to her cheek, the bruise masked behind a layer of makeup.

Without responding Alana flung Archer's hand from her own and stormed off the stage back to her dressing room. Frances Mink rushed on stage to hug Archer for a job well done, then hurried her back to change her clothes so she and her mother could meet the press together.

Alana heaved a deep sigh. The memories were interrupted as Sinclair called her name, ripping her from the moment.

"Ms. Hall? Are you alright?"

She turned her attention back to the man. "Yes, I'm fine."

Sinclair asked again. Do you want to tell me about the cotton candy?"

The woman shrugged her shoulders, pushing them up toward her pierced ears. It was a few minutes longer before she spoke, her eyes skating back and forth as if she were searching for something she couldn't find. When the words came it was as if she were updating him on the weather.

"Cotton candy was the last thing her father gave her before he left, promising to be back before she could finish it. But he never came back," Alana said with a deep sigh. "When he left me, he left her, too. Then he died a few months later," she finished, meeting his gaze before her eyes dropped to the linoleum floor.

Taking another swift breath, she shook off the moment then gestured toward the camera man who'd been standing silently off in the corner. "Are you ready, dear? Let's get this over with," she said, her somber expression shifting into a fake smile.

The man nodded, moving his equipment to where she stood, adjusting his lens to capture her best angles. He nodded at Sinclair when he was ready.

"Just say whatever comes to your mind," Ms. Hall," Sinclair said, moving behind the camera man. "Tell us whatever you want to about your relationship with Archer. "

Nodding her head Alana paused as she reached into her pocket for another cigarette. When the tobacco stick was lit, and she'd drawn one puff, blowing the smoke out of her lungs, she continued, looking directly into the camera. "Archer was special. I knew from the moment she was born that she was going to do great things. She made me a better person and I loved my daughter. I loved her very much. I just didn't do a good job of showing her how much."

THREE

The interview with the young woman's mother had been less than interesting. Sinclair knew that Alana Hall hadn't been at all forthcoming about their very volatile relationship, the likes of which had become much fodder for the tabloids. Intriguing had come though when he'd met a lengthy list of Alana Hall's former assistants and Archer's long-time nanny.

Sinclair had ascertained from his initial telephone conversation with Frances Mink, that there had been no love loss between her and the senior Ms. Hall. In fact, within the first five minutes of speaking to him, Frances Mink had expressed her disdain for the woman in words that left little to the imagination. Six other former employees had expressed the same sentiments, so he'd been anxious to meet the woman in person, considering she had lasted longer than all the others employed by the family. When Sinclair arrived at her Mt. Pleasant, New York home, she'd been more than ready to spill every secret she knew about Alana Hall and her daughter Archer.

"Would you like a cup of hot tea?" Frances Mink asked, her fragile hands balancing a kettle of hot water between her slim fingers.

"Thank you," Sinclair responded, "that would be very nice."

The woman turned to fill two porcelain cups with fluid, chatting easily as she did. "I hated that job more than I've ever hated anything in my entire life," she was saying as she dipped two Lipton teabags into steaming water. "But I loved that baby girl. She was the only reason I stayed for as long as I did."

"I'm told that she and her mother did not have a good relationship," Sinclair interjected.

Frances shook her grey head. "Those two in a room together was like having two mean alley cats trapped in a canvas bag. They were vicious to each other. Archer learned it from her mother though. That woman was evil from start to finish. But my baby girl gave it back as hard or harder than she got it."

"Were they always like that or did it start after Archer began performing?"

Frances joined him at the kitchen table, gently setting a cup of tea in front of him. She reached for a small plate of sugar cookies and pushed them in his direction. Then she continued.

"Archer was only a baby when her father hired me to be her nanny. He knew the girl's mother was plumb crazy and since he was always on the road traveling he needed someone to keep an eye on things.

"For the most part things were fine right up until Archer started to walk and talk. She was headstrong and spirited from day one and she challenged her mother at every turn. I ran interference as best I could but when she started slapping that baby around..." The woman's voice trailed off as she seemed to drift into thought.

Sinclair studied her reflection, noting the light that had dimmed ever so slightly in her dark eyes. "So, Alana Hall abused Archer?" he questioned, his gaze locking with hers.

Frances nodded. "You couldn't leave them alone together. It didn't faze her in the least to raise her hands to that child. And the least little thing would set her off. She'd get mad at Archer for asking for candy."

"How did they keep it secret for so long?"

"Most of the employees had to sign confidentiality agreements. And Ms. Hall paid everybody else off to keep quiet."

"So why are you telling me now?" Sinclair asked, curious.

"Ms. Hall didn't hire me. Archer's father did. My loyalty was to his daughter, not her mother."

"How long were you with the family?"

Frances smiled ever so slightly, lifting her teacup to her thin lips. She took a sip of her drink and set the cup back down. "Archer was sixteen when I was terminated."

"Her father had been dead for a few years though, correct?"

"That's right. But Ms. Hall kept me on since I was the only one who could handle Archer."

"Then she fired you when Archer was sixteen?"

The old woman chuckled. "No, dear, it wasn't Alana who let me go. It was Archer who fired me," she said, settling back in her seat to tell him the story.

"Excuse me," Frances Mink intoned, her disgust echoing in her frail voice. "But what are you doing?" she asked, her question directed at the lanky man standing in the doorway as he blatantly stared at a half-dressed Archer.

"Uh...I...it..."

From the center of the room, Archer laughed as a seamstress took her measurements. The stylist standing beside the woman was taking notes, both oblivious to the handyman who'd been vulgarly eyeing the young girl.

Archer spun toward the doorway, her hands propped on her slim hips as she pushed her newly blossomed, bare breasts in their direction. "Yeah, pervert, what are you doing?" the girl repeated, amusement tinting her tone.

A brilliant shade of flaming red heated the man's face as he looked from Archer to the woman and back again.

Frances slammed her hand into the center of his chest. "I'm calling the police," she said as she pushed with all her might sending him off balance. The stranger fell back into the hallway, tripping hard against the wall. "Sorry...I didn't mean...sorry," he sputtered as he turned and hurried in the opposite direction.

From inside the room Archer was laughing hysterically, clearly amused. Frances couldn't find the humor and said so. "Archer, what do you think you're doing? Why would you expose yourself to that man like that?"

Archer shrugged her shoulders, still laughing. "What's the big deal?"

"You are only sixteen-years old. That's the big deal. Your mother would have a fit if she found out..."

The younger girl interrupted. "My *mother*," she spat, the word flying out of her mouth as if it were bitter, "would have ignored it, just like she does everything else. Why are you irritating me?"

"Watch your tone, young lady," Frances said, her own hands now pressed firmly to her own hips. "You know I will not put up with you being so disrespectful."

Archer rolled her eyes. She fanned her hand toward the seamstress, dismissing the two women who'd stood silently observing, neither offering an opinion or an explanation for what Frances had just interrupted.

Stepping off the pedestal, Archer reached for a pack of Black and Milds.

"Put that down, Archer. You know you can't smoke," Frances said, snatching the cigarillo from her hand.

"I can do whatever I want," the girl said, raising her voice in defiance.

Frances took a deep breath. "No. You can't, and definitely not on my watch."

"I really have had about enough of you and your..." Archer started, just as her mother entered the room.

"What the hell is it now with you, Archer?" Alana asked, her gaze skating to her daughter and back. "Everyone's outside talking. You both know better."

Archer rolled her eyes skyward, pursing her lips tightly together.

"Why are you not dressed?" Alana asked, still waiting for one or the other to speak.

Archer tossed her mother an annoyed glare.

"Put your clothes on, Archer," Frances said, passing a terry bathrobe to the girl.

"One of you needs to answer my questions," Alana shouted, her quick fuse igniting.

"There's nothing wrong, Ms. Hall," Frances said. "Is there, Archer?" she questioned, her hand out, palm up, as she gestured for Archer to drop the smoke pack into it.

Complying, Archer shrugged her shoulders. "If you say so," she muttered under her breath, stomping toward her bedroom.

When she was out of sight, her mother cussed, directing her venom at the caregiver. "If you can't keep her in check I'll find someone who will. Do you understand me?"

Frances Hall nodded her head slowly. "Yes, ma'am," she answered, meeting the woman's gaze evenly. "Archer will be just fine."

"Fine, my ass," Alana muttered moving back to the door. "Just deal with her."

An hour later, Frances made her way to check on Archer, noting that the child was late for her tutoring session. With private tutors traveling with them to school the girl while she and her mother were touring, it was necessary to keep Archer on task, the teenager always making it a battle to get her to keep up with her studies. Frances called Archer's name before pushing open the bedroom door. "Archer…"

Archer lay across the luxurious, king-size bed with the handyman from earlier eagerly fondling her youthful breasts. The front of his khaki work pants bulged for attention as Archer toyed with the man's emotions. She was giggling as if she were excited by his touch, encouraging his ministrations. Both jumped, startled, as Frances pushed her way inside.

"Oh, hell no!" the older woman exclaimed when she caught sight of them. She reached for the intercom system on the wall. "I need security," she shouted into the monitor, calling for help.

"She invited me…" the intruder started, pointing a finger in Archer's direction.

"Child molester!" Archer exclaimed as she pulled herself upright against the headboard. "He made me do it!"

Raging into the room Frances slammed an open palm against the man's face, slapping him harshly. Before she could slap him a second time, two armed guards came storming in behind her. "Get him out of here," she ordered.

As the two employees hauled the man from the room, Frances slammed the door closed behind them. She spun back on her heels to confront Archer, her body shaking with fury.

"What has gotten into you? You don't let some stranger manhandle you like that, Archer. I taught you better than that."

"I didn't do anything," Archer shouted back, tears swelling in her large eyes.

Frances closed her own eyes, taking a deep inhale of oxygen. When she opened them, Archer's tears had begun to roll over her the high bones of her cheeks.

"I didn't do anything," Archer repeated.

Frances dropped down onto the side of the bed, reaching to wrap Archer in a warm embrace. She held the girl tightly, then pressed a damp kiss against her forehead.

Almost overnight Archer had gone from being an innocent little girl to a blossoming young woman. She'd inherited her mother's curvaceous figure and she was not lacking for male attention. Most of her admirers had to be reminded that she was still very much a child, despite what Archer might have wanted. Frances had had to lecture the girl more times than should have been necessary about maintaining her virtue, when so many were trying to take advantage of her naivety.

Clutching Archer by the shoulders Frances held the girl at arm's length, meeting her tearful stare. "You did do something, Archer and you know that what you did was wrong. I can't protect you, baby girl, if I can't trust you to do what's right."

Archer stiffened with teenage indignation. "I don't need your protection. I don't need anything from you. You are not my mother," she hissed harshly.

Frances heaved a deep sigh. "No. I'm not your mother. *I* want what's best for you. If you don't see that then I don't need to be here."

"Go then," Archer said, snatching herself from the woman's clutch. "Just go. I don't care if you're here or not."

Frances opened her mouth to speak just as they were interrupted yet again by Archer's mother.

"What the hell is going on?" Alana said, the bedroom door slamming harshly against the wall. "Why is there a police car in the driveway? I told you to handle her," she shouted directly at Frances.

Archer jumped to her feet, standing toe to toe with her mother. "I don't need anyone to handle me. I need you all to leave me the hell alone. Just go to..."

Before the next expletive was out of her daughter's mouth, Alana slapped Archer harshly. Eyes widened, Archer suddenly slapped her mother back. Alana stood stunned, her palm flying to the side of her face to caress the stinging flesh.

She pointed a finger in Frances' direction. "This is all your fault," she shouted.

Unable to fathom how things had gotten so out of hand Frances pushed her way between the two women. She gripped Archer's arm, her head shaking from side to side. "Archer," she started.

"No! Get out. You're fired," Archer shouted. "I don't want you here anymore. "Get out!"

Frances looked from Archer to her mother and back. "Archer, please calm..."

Still incensed, Archer snapped a second time. "I said get out! Get out before I have you thrown out!"

"It's about time," Alana sneered, pushing Frances away from her daughter. "You heard her. You're fired. I'll have my attorney send you your severance package, but I want you off the property today."

Frances stepped back, her head still waving from side to side. Saying nothing, the woman nodded her compliance, then turned abruptly and exited the room.

Throwing herself against her bed, Archer burst into tears, sobbing helplessly.

Standing over her, Alana stared, her hand still pressed to the side of her face. With nothing else left to say, she too exited the room, closing the door easily behind her.

Sinclair was jotting notes as fast as Frances Mink could speak, not wanting to miss a single word of the woman's reflections. When she suddenly stopped talking, he looked up with a start. The matriarch was smiling ever so slightly, a look of contentment crossing her face.

She rose from her seat, moving out of the room and returning before he could think to question what might be on her mind. She carried a large box in her hands and gestured for him to relieve her of the weight.

"What's all this?" Sinclair asked curiously.

"Letters from Archer. When I first left, Archer wrote me every day. At first, she kept begging me to come back, but I couldn't. I'd had enough. Now I get a letter from her every month, postcards when she travels, plus presents at Christmas, on my birthday, and Mother's Day."

"She loves you."

"I love her. Archer was the daughter I couldn't have. But she wasn't my child and when she and her mother both had no problems reminding me of that, I knew that it was time for a change."

Sinclair nodded. "Why did you agree to speak with me? Everyone else I've spoken to is more intent on hurting Archer than helping her. So why are you speaking with me and not the tabloids for compensation?"

Frances dropped back down against the padded chair seat. She flipped through the mass of envelopes in the box, pulling one from the back of the collection. "This is the last letter Archer wrote me. I think you'll find it very interesting," she said as she passed the correspondence to him.

Sinclair eyed her curiously as he pulled the length of pale blue paper scented with lavender from the ivory mailer. The handwriting was neat and even, the letters curving gracefully across the paper in bright blue ink. He glanced up at Frances who had risen to clear the table, then back down to the letter in his hand, beginning to read it slowly.

Dear Minky,

The tour is almost over, and I am more than ready. I can't begin to tell you how exhausted I am. The last album is still at the top of the charts though so no complaints there.

I hope everything is well with you. I miss you, Minky, and want you to promise to come see me when I get back to California. Or I can come see you. Did I tell you how much I miss you?

New news! There's a filmmaker who is going to do the Archer story for HBO. It's supposed to be one of those tell-all exposés about my rise to fame. I gave him your name, so he will probably call you to talk. Tell him everything for me, Minky. Please. It's time everyone knew the truth. That nothing about my life has been as perfect as we all pretended it was.

By the way, he's a beautiful man! Tall, dark, and handsome. The kind of man I would fantasize about when I was a little girl, remember? The only thing missing is the white horse! Hahaha! Seriously though, what I liked most about him was that he seemed very genuine. He made me laugh and he was very sweet. I'm not sure why I trust him, but I do. I can't remember the last time I trusted any man. Is that crazy of me, Minky?

His name is Sinclair Cooper. You'll know him when you see him. He'll be the beautiful man with the smiling eyes. I'm sure he'll make you laugh, too!

I love you, Minky. Please take care of yourself until I see you again. XOXO, Archer

Sinclair read the letter once and then a second time. He felt himself smiling ever so slightly, aware that Frances had stopped what she was doing to watch him. He met her intense stare.

"You were right. It is interesting," he said, trying to keep his voice as casual as he could.

Frances smiled back, chuckling ever so softly. "Everything with my girl Archer usually is, Mr. Cooper! Good luck when you go back to California."

FOUR

"I can't believe she let you read my letters!" Archer said with a deep laugh. The color had risen to her cheeks tinting them a deep shade of red. "I thought Minky had my back!" she exclaimed.

"Clearly Mrs. Minks is very fond of you."

Archer turned to stare out the passenger window of Sinclair's car. They were traveling from her home in Cambria to his cabin at Big Bear Lake in the back woods of the San Bernardino State Forest, about one hundred miles northeast of Los Angeles. The five-hour trek had started quietly, Archer finishing out that nap she'd been so desperate for.

For the first hour, she'd snored. Loudly. Her head tossed back against the back seat where she'd chosen to sprawl the length of her body, professing she would be more comfortable.

Santa Barbara had been the midway point of their ride and when he'd stopped for gas, and food, she'd woken refreshed, seemingly excited, and chatty. Moving to the front seat she had been regaling him with stories from her childhood ever since, filling in the blanks others had omitted.

"I would not have wished a child like me on my worst enemy," Archer finally said, turning from the window to stare at him. "I was horrible!"

"From everything I know you had a lot of challenges. Constantly traveling and touring with your mother didn't afford you much of a childhood," Sinclair said. "It also didn't help that your mother is a piece of work, too!"

Archer shifted her gaze back out the window. Since the paparazzi had uncovered the illicit relationship between Alana and Paulo, she'd been having a hard time reconciling her feelings for the woman. Her emotions wafted between hatred and pity, unable to understand what motivated her mother to be so evil.

Sinclair read her mind. "It's okay to be angry with her," he said softly. "What she has done to you is unfathomable. A lesser woman would not have handled herself so regally."

"Let's not talk about my mother," Archer said, having no interest in trying to make sense out of nonsense.

Sinclair nodded his agreement, allowing the subject of Alana Hall to die, if only for the moment.

Silence billowed full and thick through the vehicle as each fell into their own thoughts. Archer appreciated his understanding despite knowing he wanted to know more. It was his job to investigate and he had questions. Putting them aside for the moment, to let her collect herself, spoke volumes as far as she was concerned.

She changed the subject. "Let's talk about you," she said. "You know a lot about me, Sinclair Cooper, but I don't know anything at all about you."

Sinclair cut his eyes in her direction, then shifted his attention back to the road. He was not a man accustomed to talking about himself. Nor was he one to answer a lot of questions about his life. He felt comfortable asking the questions, not being expected to give answers to them. Archer's sudden request put him at odds with what he was there to do, because he was there to explore her life, not his own.

He shrugged his broad shoulders. "There's nothing to tell."

"So, you're not an open book?"

A slight smile pulled at his full lips. "I'm probably a lot of things, but definitely not that. Is that going to be a problem for you?"

Archer pondered his question for a moment. "Not really. It might come up again if I decide to sleep with you though. I usually like to know a little something about the men I bed."

Sinclair laughed. "I didn't realize that's an option that was on the table."

"Don't tell me you haven't thought about taking me to bed. Haven't your heard? Every male between the ages of fourteen and eighty-four has fantasized about having sex with me. There was an article about it in some magazine a few years ago. Billboard or Playboy or one of the others. I don't remember which."

"Does it bother you that the public sexualizes you the way they do? Because you have really gone the distance not to sexualize yourself. You never dress provocatively. Your performances are always the epitome of taste and refinement. None of your songs are explicit. In fact, the image you project is quite the opposite."

"Honestly? I could really care less. I know who I am, and I know what my values are. People do and say what makes them feel important. I just won't play into it. Since I lost my virginity, I can count on one hand how many men can say they've had a taste of all this," she said as she gestured down the length of her body with her hands. "And I'd have fingers left over. I'm very discerning about my sexual partners."

"So, sleeping with me isn't an option that's on the table?"

Archer laughed, noting the amusement that danced in his dark eyes.

There was a moment that passed between them, their comfort levels rising another few degrees. Both fell into the heat of it, allowing themselves to enjoy what was becoming a fast friendship.

"I haven't had a lot of partners either," Sinclair said, breaking the silence that had draped between them like a cashmere blanket. "No serious relationships anyway. I've never been married or engaged. I've always been focused on my work. My films have been my lovers and my career the love of my life."

Archer nodded. "But you do have sex?"

He laughed. "Occasionally."

"I'm just checking," she said., giggling softly.

For the rest of the trip their conversation was easy-going and comfortable. Archer discovered he had a penchant for old black and white movies and mystery novels. He ate fast foods, In-N-Out Burger mostly, more than he cooked. He also proclaimed himself extremely anal and a bit of a germaphobe.

His friends all called him *Sin* for short, because of the things they imagined him doing and not necessarily what he'd actually done. He'd been a bit of a rebel in his younger days and his reputation had stuck. She latched on to that piece of knowledge with both hands.

"Sin! I like that. I really like that! That is so fitting!"

"How so?" Sinclair questioned.

"You look like sin!"

He chuckled, his head waving from side to side. "What does sin look like?"

Archer bit down against her bottom lip, pausing for a moment to ponder the question.

"Like Friday night when you're sixteen and your parents are gone for the weekend."

He smiled as she continued.

"Or when a guy takes you shopping with his Black card and you know exactly what he expects after but you're already plotting how not to give it to him. Or when you tell your best friend the brownies are all gone but you've got the plate, a gallon of ice cream and one spoon hidden in your bedroom."

Sinclair laughed. "I look like all that?"

"You look like every perverted thought that goes through a woman's mind when she sees a beautiful man and imagines them spending a weekend together while she leaves the kids and a husband home alone."

"You have a vivid imagination," he said with a soft chuckle.

"It's why I'm a brilliant songwriter."

He nodded.

"Did I offend you?" she asked when he fell silent, saying nothing for the next ten miles.

He cut his eyes in her direction and shook his head. "No, not at all. I find you quite amusing, Archer."

"Call me Arch. All my friends do."

He smiled. "I'm glad you're thinking of me as a friend."

"Me, too. Right now, besides Minky, you're the only one I have."

"I find that hard to believe. I would think you have a wonderful inner circle of friends who support you."

"Clearly, you still need to do your homework." She shook her head and her voice dropped an octave. "It's hard for me to trust that people have my best interests at heart. Everyone always wants something from me. I don't know what it is to just hang out with a group of women and not have everyone expecting me to pick up the tab or let them follow me around like puppies because they think I need an entourage. The last *friend* I had lied to me, multiple times, and now every time I turn around she's talking about me behind my back. Plus," she concluded, taking a deep breath before speaking. "Although it's not widely known, I have mean girl tendencies."

Sinclair nodded. "I'm sorry," he said.

Archer shrugged. "I have great hair dressers though. That counts for something, I'm sure."

Sinclair reached out and took her hand beneath his as he held onto the steering wheel with the other. He entwined his fingers between hers. Archer closed her eyes and allowed herself to savor the sensation of his touch, his palm gently grazing hers. As she opened her eyes she turned her head to stare back out the window. Neither said another word for the remainder of the drive.

The newly remodeled, lakefront estate was absolutely divine. The log cabin home sat on two exceptionally green acres with amazing mountain views in the distance and close to two-hundred feet of lake frontage. There were seven bedrooms and four full bathrooms, rock fireplaces, vaulted, open-beam ceilings, a gourmet kitchen and a boathouse. The brother was clearly living large despite his efforts to appear unassuming, Archer thought as he gave her a tour and told her to make herself at home.

He dropped her luggage onto a queen-sized bed in one of the guest bedrooms. The space was warm and inviting with its hand-hewn logs, reading nook in a window seat, and rock fireplace.

"I need to grab a shower," he said, "and maybe a thirty-minute nap. Afterward we can figure out what to do for supper and discuss what's going to happen when we get started tomorrow morning."

Archer nodded. "Thank you," she said, her voice a loud whisper.

Her soft tone stirred something in his midsection that he didn't quite recognize. Sinclair nodded, gave her a slight wink of his eye and then he disappeared down the length of hallway to the master bedroom.

Archer listened as he moved around in the back, sounding like he was throwing things about as he looked for something. Then he closed the door and the house filled with silence.

She moved back to the home's common areas. He was a minimalist, the décor exceptionally sparse. A sofa, two chairs and a coffee table filled the living room. The furniture was mismatched and well-worn, but it worked. There was an abundance of pillows and throw blankets tossed about that made the space feel extremely comfortable.

A dining table that sat four was positioned in one corner near the kitchen and there was a baby grand piano dead center of what was supposed to be the dining room. She trailed her fingers across the keys and smiled.

Stacks of books were piled atop the coffee table, the kitchen table, and the counters. Books, camera equipment, assorted notepads and pens. She was surprised to see that he sporadically left notes all over the house, jotting down whatever might come to him wherever he might be standing. Her name was scribbled on pads in the kitchen, the living room, the bedroom, even the bathroom, in handwriting that was less than stellar. Archer made a mental note to give him a hard time about his penmanship because she couldn't read half of what he'd written.

She moved into the kitchen with its high-end appliances, center island and marble counters. His cabinets, pantry and freezer were well stocked which surprised her. Clearly someone liked to cook, and he had already shared that it wasn't one of his strengths.

And hour later, she was putting the finishing touches on a peach cobbler. A large pan of macaroni and cheese was baking in the oven and she'd thrown beef spare ribs into a brand new Instant Pot pressure cooker that he'd never used. She moved back to the freezer for a bag of green beans. When she turned around Sinclair was standing in the middle of the kitchen peering into the oven.

Startled, she jumped, the bag in her hand falling to the floor. "You scared the crap out of me," she snapped, drawing her hand to her heart.

"Sorry," Sinclair responded as he held up his own hands in surrender.

"Do you always tiptoe around in your own house?"

Sinclair laughed, glancing down to his bare feet. "Didn't know that was what I was doing."

Archer's eyes followed his. He had large feet. Exceptionally large feet, long and wide with really cute toes. He wiggled them, and the gesture drew her eyes back to his face. They both laughed heartily.

"You cook?" he asked moving back to peer into the oven. "It smells amazing in here!"

She nodded. "I love to cook. It actually relaxes me. I don't do it often unfortunately because it's usually just me."

"Didn't you cook for Paulo?"

"My ex-husband preferred to eat out so that he could be seen. He hated my cooking. Actually, he hated me now that I think about it."

"Hate is pretty harsh don't you think?"

"You don't do what he did, to someone you like or care about. And you definitely don't do it someone you love."

"Well, I haven't eaten it yet but I'm pretty sure I'm going to love your cooking!"

Archer smiled. "I'm impressed with how well stocked your kitchen is."

"Courtesy of my mother. She insists on it and usually she's the only one who cooks for me."

"I think I'm going to like your mother."

He leaned back against the counter as he watched her prep a green bean casserole, dropping the vegetables into a pot of boiling water until they were almost done. Salt, pepper, a can of cream of mushroom soup and French-fried onions for the topping completed the dish. When she popped it into the oven to lightly toast the top he shook his head.

"That actually looked easy."

"It is. That's why you should cook and not eat fast food. This is far better for you. Maybe tomorrow I can run to the store and get some fresh vegetables which would be even better."

"We will put it on our list!"

"If you set the table we can eat in about ten minutes."

Sinclair gave her a slight salute. "Yes, ma'am." He moved to the cabinet and pulled out plates and then silverware from a kitchen drawer.

Archer tossed him a look, her eyes darting back and forth so that it wasn't too obvious that she was staring.

He had changed into a pair of sweat pants and a V-necked tee shirt. The casual attire accentuated his athletic frame, showcasing his broad chest and thick arms nicely. He smelled like vanilla and cocoa butter, remnants of the body wash he'd used. She inhaled him as he swept past her, moving to the dining table. Heat pulsed through her midsection sending a volt of energy through her feminine spirit. She took another deep breath and held it for a moment before blowing it slowly past her lips. Desire surged, and it was unexpected and disconcerting.

She shook the sensation from her spirit as she checked on the food. "So," she said, needing conversation to distract her from her thoughts. "Why do you have a piano in the dining room? Do you play?"

Sinclair laughed. "My mother is Roberta Cooper."

She paused, her neck snapping as she turned to look at him. "Roberta Cooper the jazz pianist?"

He nodded. "The one and only. She insisted on having a piano here when she visits, and I didn't need a formal dining room set."

Archer stared at him, a wooden spoon paused in midair. "Is there anything else about you that I should probably know?"

He laughed. "Did you really need to know who my mother was?"

"I adore your mother. I have all her albums. I learned how to play the piano because of your mother."

"I'll have to remember to tell her that."

Archer rolled her eyes skyward. "You're killing me, Sin!"

He laughed again. "It's not that big a deal."

"That's because she's *your* mother. For me she's the mother I wished I had!"

He shrugged his wide shoulders, a hint of something Archer couldn't define washing over his expression. "Maybe."

"I know you play, right? I can't imagine Roberta Cooper being your mother and you not knowing how to play the piano."

"I was six when she started to teach me, but I wasn't good about practicing. My sister is much better than I am."

"Yeah! You play," Archer said as she grabbed the dish of macaroni with an oven mitt and carried it to the table.

"I know where to put my fingers on the keys that's about all."

"I don't believe that for one minute. After dinner you're going to have to play for me."

He moved to her side and grabbed the plate of cornbread as she pulled the green bean casserole from the oven.

"Why don't you just play for me instead? I don't see any need for me to embarrass myself." He winked an eye at her and the gesture made her smile.

When the food was on the table the two sat down, Sinclair eyeing the meal excitedly. It had been a minute since his last home cooked meal and admittedly, he thoroughly enjoyed good food. He bowed his head and said a quick prayer of thanksgiving.

It was only as he reached for the large spoon perched in the macaroni that he realized Archer was staring at him intently. Her gaze was misted and the look in her eyes suddenly pulled at his heartstrings.

"I'm sorry, did I do something?" he asked, a wave of confusion crossing his face.

Archer shook her head. "You're the first man I've been around who has prayed over his food. Minky makes me say grace when I'm with her but my mother wasn't big on prayer, church or God."

He nodded. "I pray. And I have a praying mother. It makes a difference."

Archer nodded, then closed her eyes and lowered her head as she whispered her own blessing skyward. When she looked back up he was smiling at her.

"You can cook!" Sinclair exclaimed as he savored the first bites of his food. He sucked meat off the bone, those beef ribs perfectly seasoned and melt-in-your-mouth tender.

Archer grinned, her smile abundant as she took the first bite of her own spoonful of macaroni.

They both ate with gusto, realizing the meal was a first for them that day. Conversation was nominal, just polite chatter as they enjoyed their food. When both of their plates were empty, Archer politely excused herself to go check the cobbler that was browning nicely in the oven.

"All we're missing is a little ice cream," she said as she moved back to her seat.

"Did you check the deep freeze in the garage?"

Archer blinked, her eyes narrowing ever so slightly. "You have another freezer in the garage?"

Sinclair laughed. "My mother believes in being prepared. She's slightly crazy," he said teasingly. He rose from his own seat and seconds later returned with two containers of ice cream in hand. "Vanilla and butter pecan! Will this work?" he asked as he gestured with one and then the other.

"I *really* like your mother!" Archer exclaimed as she clapped her hands together. Her excitement was registered all over her face, her eyes dancing with joy.

Minutes later she had dished up bowls of warm cobbler topped with large scoops of vanilla ice cream. Sinclair carried both bowls to the sofa and gestured for her to join him. He'd turned on the stereo and one of his mother's albums played in the background. The music was teasing and sultry and befitting the mood between them that seemed to rise out of nowhere.

They sat listening for a good long while and then Sinclair broke the silence.

"When did you know your marriage was over?"

Archer had been staring out into space, the question totally unexpected. She turned to stare at him, pondering his query for a moment.

"I'm sure you know we snuck off and got married in Bermuda at the Registrar's office, while Paulo was on hiatus from his television show."

Sinclair nodded. "Yes. Your fans were completely taken by surprise. I don't think anyone knew you two were even dating. At least not seriously."

"We weren't. We were friends but not much more than that. It was really a spur of the moment decision that seemed right after too much black rum. I knew we were doomed when the Registrar told us marriage was not to be entered into lightly."

"So why didn't you just say no and walk away?"

Archer blew a soft sigh, her mind seeming to race back to a time and place she had hoped to forget. The stress of it furrowed her brow as she struggled to find the words to explain. "I wanted it to work," she said finally, "and I truly believed that if we made an earnest effort that it could."

"And Paulo?"

"Paulo sobered up and remembered that he still had wild oats to sow. He went back to sleeping around with anything in a skirt that talked to him."

"I guess it's hard to maintain a relationship when your spouse isn't committed."

She shrugged. "It's virtually impossible, but I only have myself to blame."

"Have you ever been in love, Arch?" he asked, his gaze meeting hers evenly. "With anyone?"

Archer stared at him, her gaze doing an easy two-step with his. She smiled and then she rose from her seat, gathered the dirty dishes and moved back to the kitchen. She didn't respond, and Sinclair didn't push, feeling like he already knew the answer.

FIVE

Arch made herself comfortable in the window seat that looked out over the dense forest of land bordering the property. She pulled a cotton blanket tightly around her torso and pulled her knees to her chest as she leaned back against the cushions. Sinclair had retired to his own bedroom hours earlier, but she hadn't been able to fall asleep.

Tired of tossing and turning she'd tiptoed back out to the living room and had made herself comfortable. There had been much for her to process. Most particularly the predicament she suddenly found herself in the midst of.

She liked Sinclair Cooper. She liked him a lot. He was kind and clearly had a generous spirit. He made her laugh and he had no qualms about laughing at himself. The time they'd spent together had renewed her faith in men because she surely had been feeling some way about the male species. She was rational enough to know she couldn't judge all men by the actions of Paulo. But Paulo had left a bitter taste in her mouth where any man was concerned.

Sinclair, however, gave her hope. He also excited her, and it had been some time since any man had her feeling giddy. But the more she thought about him, and her, and the possibility of a them, the more she knew such was well out of the realms of possibility.

Whether she admitted it aloud, or not, Archer knew she was a complete and total mess. She could pretend as much as she wanted that her early morning episode had been an accident, and maybe on some level it was. But if she were honest with herself, what she claimed to have been an accident, had been a cry for help and she didn't know how to begin to make that happen.

Archer had been angry, out of control and tired of pretending all was well when it wasn't. Over the years she had mastered the art of pretending. Of laughing and joking, even flirting, to detract attention from how unhappy she was. She'd been doing it to hide her pain since she was a child. And even though hurting herself hadn't been her objective, she had desperately wanted the pain she felt to go away for good.

She blew a soft sigh. The man they called Sin was one of the good guys. He surely didn't deserve the designer luggage she was toting, unpacked baggage festering deeply below the surface of her spirit.

She sat staring. There was a lake in the distance and the sliver of moonlight reflecting off the surface danced with the gentle sway of the water. As she sat quietly with herself, her mind churning it all over and over again, Archer could hear Minky's voice admonishing her to pray her troubles away.

Pray it away, Arch, her caregiver had often extolled. *Pray it away!* But despite her best efforts Archer couldn't find the words to tell God what was hurting her heart.

Sinclair debated whether he should go check on Archer, or not. He had heard her room door open, but it had never closed. He'd been listening intently, noting her footsteps against the hardwood floors and then quiet as they'd faded off into the distance.

There was a part of him that thought he should be concerned. Memories of how he'd found her that morning haunted him. Despite her protests that nothing was wrong, and the moment had been an accident he sensed that Archer Santana had issues that were larger than she was willing to admit or that he was able to handle.

He had heard her crying in the shower, a low mournful sob that had pulled at his heartstrings. He had wanted to go to her, but their relationship still had many boundaries. He instinctively knew that in that moment, even the act of consoling her would have been too intimate for them both.

He appreciated that they had been able to find a comfortable balance with each other. He sensed that there was much about Archer that he had yet to explore. He had only begun to peel her many layers away and a part of him was worried about what he might find. But there was something about Archer that moved his spirit. He was rooting for her success and a bigger part of him wanted to be a part of whatever that success looked like.

There was no denying his attraction to her. It sprung to full and abundant attention each time she was near. Because Archer Santana was a stunning beauty. She had skin like polished marble, her warm complexion reminding him of melted dark chocolate. Her almond-shaped eyes were deep pools of black ice and her mouth begged to be kissed. She was model-thin with a hint of curve in all the right places and everything about her left him hard and wanting. Fighting those feelings was quickly becoming his biggest challenge.

He blew a heavy sigh as he pondered his next move. Despite the work they still had to do, the hard questions he knew he would ask, he worried about her. He questioned whether she would be up for what he would demand from her because he fully intended to take her where she had often refused to go. She'd promised him complete and total transparency and he fully intended to hold her to that.

He rose from his bed and moved to the door. He paused, listening intently and then he pulled it open and headed back to the living room.

Archer sat on the piano bench. Her hands danced across the piano keys, the soft tinkling of notes moving Sinclair to smile. A notebook rested on the music rack and she paused to jot down something, then returned to playing. Her eyes were closed, and her head swayed from side to side.

He stood watching, the sweetness of the tune sweeping around the room. He closed his own eyes and allowed himself to settle into what was clearly a moment of creativity, Archer's talent abundant.

There was an abrupt pause and when he opened his eyes, she was staring at him.

"I'm sorry. I didn't mean to wake you," she said, their gazes locking.

He shook his head. "You didn't. I couldn't sleep."

Archer nodded. "Must be something in the water," she said as she gave him a slight smile.

"Don't let me interrupt. That was very pretty. Something new?"

Her smile widened. "I call it *Something About Sin*."

Sinclair laughed. "I'm glad I could be a source of inspiration for you."

"Me, too!"

He moved to the sofa and sat down. "Do you mind if I sit and listen?" he asked.

"There was a moment of hesitation and then she shrugged. She closed her notebook and began to play.

He smiled recognizing her most recent Billboard hit, the song topping the charts at number one. When she hit the song's hook he realized he was humming along with her.

Archer grinned. "You have a very nice voice, Sin."

He bowed his head in appreciation. "I can hold a tune, but it's nowhere near as nice as yours. You've got serious pipes, Arch!"

"It's a gift and one I try not to take for granted. She rose from the bench and moved to the empty seat beside him.

"I should let you get back to it," he said, suddenly feeling anxious by the nearness of her. Heat wafted through his lower quadrant and settled in the sinewy muscles below his waist.

Archer shifted her body closer to his. She reached for his hand and guided his arm up and around her shoulders. She settled herself against him as she extended her legs along the sofa. She leaned her head against his chest.

Sinclair inhaled, a deep breath catching in his midsection. He allowed himself to settle around her, praying that she didn't notice the bulge of flesh pressing for attention against the front of his sweatpants.

Archer ran her fingers down the length of his arm, playing with the fingers on his hand. He wore a diamond-encrusted, gold band on his middle finger and she twisted it around in a circle.

"Just make yourself comfortable," he said, trying to balance a hint of sarcasm in the comment with the desire that was rising like a storm wind.

Archer laughed. "I'm not a patient woman, Sin, and I get the impression you believe in taking life slowly."

"It has its advantages."

"Maybe, and maybe you miss out on living by not being more spontaneous."

"Arch, I don't want to give you the wrong..." he started.

She pressed her index finger to his full lips, stalling his comment. "Don't make this more than it is, Sin."

"And what is it?" he asked, his soft tone filled with curiosity.

Archer squeezed his hand. "This is just a moment between good friends," she said casually. "Nothing more, nothing less."

Sinclair nodded. Archer began to hum, another song rising slowly in the late-night air. The private concert was telling, the song choices perfect for the moment and he realized Archer was as concerned about not rocking the boat they were riding as he was. But he also sensed there was something she needed and the act of simply being in his arms was fulfilling that need. In that moment she was allowing herself to be vulnerable and trusting it wouldn't blow up on her.

He pulled her closer, tightening the hold he had around her torso. Sinclair heard her breathe a sigh of relief, expelling the weight of whatever burdened her. They sat together for a good long while, talking about music and what was near and dear to her in the business. They talked, and listened, and when both grew tired, he gave her one last hug goodnight and headed back to his room as she headed to hers.

"Goodnight, Arch!"

"Goodnight, Sin."

She called his name one last time as he moved to close his room door.

"Yes?"

"Thank you," she said, her eyes smiling as she stared in his direction. And then she moved into the spare bedroom and closed the door, the echo of the lock clicking resounding through the air.

Sinclair was wide awake and moving about in the kitchen when his cell phone rang, the device vibrating loudly against the countertop. He answered on the third ring. "Hello?"

"Hey, it's me," Roman Wright responded on the other end. "Good morning."

"Good morning."

"How is she?" his friend asked.

"She's good. Still asleep I think. "

"That's good, right?"

"She needed some rest so I'm thinking it's very good."

"I'm worried about her. Things are getting messier and now the press is camped outside her New York apartment."

"New York?"

"It's the home she shared with Paulo. She's got a recording session in a few days, so they know she'll be back in the city soon."

"Well, just how much messier can it get?" Sinclair questioned.

Roman blew a heavy sigh. "Apparently there's video tape, and her mother is shopping it around hoping to sell it before it gets leaked. And Paulo announced his engagement to Lucia Ferreira."

"Wasn't she his co-star on his last movie?"

"The one and only."

"That girl's like ten-years old!"

"She just turned nineteen. They're in Greece together while all of this plays out. His people reached out about wanting to issue a joint statement, so I'm going to have to talk to her about it."

"I'm sure that will go over well," Sinclair said facetiously.

"Well, we're about to find out. Open your door. I just pulled into your driveway."

"Aren't I lucky!" Sinclair exclaimed. He moved to the front window and peered out. Roman was just stepping out of his car when a second vehicle pulled into the driveway behind him. He stood watching as Roman moved to help Ben Goodman, his camera man, with his equipment. He was at the front door to usher them inside before they stepped onto the porch.

He and Ben slapped palms and bumped shoulders in greeting.

"Good morning," Sinclair said.

"It will be as long as you have coffee," Ben answered.

Roman echoed his sentiment. "Coffee would be really good!" he said as he and Sinclair embraced. "How are you, brother-in-law?"

"I'm standing," Sinclair said as he shrugged his broad shoulders. "There's a fresh pot of coffee on the counter. I'm surprised you didn't bring that sister of mine."

"Didn't tell her I was coming. If I had, I would have had to bring her, and your mother!" he said jokingly.

"Smart man!"

Ben laughed as he pulled two cups from the cabinet and poured freshly brewed French roast into both. "So, where's our star? I'm excited to meet Ms. Santana. I'm a big fan!"

"Don't you go and get all star struck on me," Sinclair admonished. "I need you to be on top of your game today."

"Hey, you always work with the best. On top is where I stay!" The man moved to the refrigerator, peering inside. "You don't by chance have any of those pastries your mom always keeps around, do you, Sin?"

"I don't think so, but I know there are some of those frozen biscuits in the freezer."

"If one of you whips up some eggs and bacon with those biscuits I'll take a plate," Roman said as he took a sip of his coffee.

Sinclair chuckled as he shook his head. "I'll fix breakfast," he said, moving back behind the counter.

The men chatted easily as Sinclair pulled eggs and bacon from the fridge. Minutes later the bacon was beginning to sizzle in the oven, eggs were whipped in a bowl and ready for the skillet and those biscuits were just starting to brown.

The conversation revolved around football, women, football, sex, football, and women.

"I swear, your sister stays mad at me," Roman intoned.

Sinclair laughed. "I told you Kendra was special when you married her. She is her mother's daughter through and through."

"Well, had anyone told me marriage would be this hard I would have stayed single."

"We did tell you," Ben added. "You didn't want to listen. You were in love, remember?"

"He's still in love, that's why he's complaining," Sinclair said as he leaned to peer into the refrigerator, reaching for a jug of orange juice. "She's got him wrapped around her little finger and she's tightening that noose."

Ben laughed. "My brother, you have been officially whipped!"

Roman shook his head. "At least I get me some on the regular," he muttered.

Sinclair grinned, cutting an eye at his friend. "That's still my sister you're talking about. Don't make me whup your ass!"

Laughter rang abundantly around the room. As Archer moved into the space, she smiled, instantly pulled into the ease and joy of their camaraderie. "Good morning," she chimed, her gaze sweeping from one to the other.

All three men came to an abrupt pause, turning toward where she stood. Archer was wearing one of the Sinclair's white dress shirts, the oversized garment falling to just above her knees. Only two, maybe three buttons held it closed, exposing a hint of cleavage and much leg. She was barefoot, her manicured toes painted a vibrant shade of pink. Her hair was pulled into a messy, high-top ponytail and she wore no makeup, her complexion gleaming. She was breathtaking!

The quiet in the room was suddenly deafening. The three men stood with mouths open and eyes widened.

"Is it not a good morning?" she quipped, amusement dancing across her face.

Sinclair shook his head, swiping at the reverie he'd fallen into. "No...yes...I mean good morning!"

"Arch, hey!" Roman added.

"Good...good morning!" Ben said, suddenly tongue-tied.

The trio shot looks around the room, eyeing each other as they waited for one of them to take the lead.

Archer laughed. She extended her hand toward Ben. "Hi. I'm Archer, and you are...?"

"Sorry...Ben. Ben Goodman. Cameraman extraordinaire. I look forward to working with you today."

Archer gave the man a magnificent smile. "It's nice to meet you, Ben."

She moved to Roman's side, her arms open as she hugged him. "How's it going, Mr. Manager?"

Roman nodded as he hugged her back. "It's all good. How are you doing, Arch?" he asked, genuine concern in his tone.

Archer shrugged her shoulders. "I guess that all depends on who you ask." She smiled sweetly and then shifted the conversation. "Were you able to get my window fixed?"

"Like new! It's all handled so there's nothing for you to worry about."

"I wasn't worried." She turned her attention toward Sinclair, moving to his side. Their gazes connected and held, a moment passing between them that didn't include the other two men.

Sinclair bit down against his bottom lip, his intoxicating stare like a rod of heat, searing and intense. "Good morning," he said again. "How'd you sleep?"

"I haven't slept that well in a long time. That mattress is wonderful!"

He reached a hand out and slid his fingers along the lapel of his shirt that she wore.

Archer's bright smile widened. "It was hanging in the closet, so I borrowed it. I didn't think you'd mind," she said softly.

He smiled back. "Not at all. It actually looks better on you than it does on me."

She suddenly gestured toward the oven. "Two more seconds and those biscuits are going to be burnt. And you should probably check on that bacon, too!"

Sinclair snapped to attention, cussing as he rushed to grab an oven mitt

Archer chuckled warmly. "I should go change," she said as she blessed each of them with one last glance.

With two hot pans in hand Sinclair looked back up to stare after her, watching the easy sway of her hips as she glided away.

He dropped the pans onto the stove top and quickly transferred the biscuits to a serving dish. The bacon had crisped perfectly, and he plated that as well.

Behind him, Ben cleared his throat. Loudly. "You hit that!" he exclaimed, something like reverence washing over his expression. He raised both hands as if surrendering and pretended to bow, shifting back and forth. "You so hit that! You are my hero!"

Roman moved onto his feet. He'd turned a brilliant shade of red and looked like his head was about to explode. "Please, tell me you did not sleep with her. She does not need any more scandal on the front pages of every news rag around the world. All I've been doing lately is putting out media fires!"

Sinclair shook his head, his eyes rolling skyward. "I did not sleep with her," he hissed between clenched teeth. "You know me better than that."

Roman continued. "She is just too fragile right now. And dammit, I trusted you to take care of her!

Sinclair snapped. "I said, I didn't sleep with her," he repeated, his voice rising. The look he gave his friend was cold, edged in emotion that suddenly had Roman backpedaling.

"What I meant was I care about both of you. I don't doubt that..."

"Sin was a perfect gentleman," Archer interjected, moving back into the room. "I can vouch for him," she said, the faintest hint of sarcasm in her tone. "But I'm also a grown ass woman who can decide for herself what she wants. I had a father, Roman, and you're not him. But I do appreciate your concern."

All three men turned toward her, each feeling slightly foolish. Archer had changed into a pair of yoga pants and a tank top. She moved to the coffee pot and poured herself a cup.

"Is breakfast ready?" she asked. And then she turned toward the dining table, tossing Sinclair a wink of her eye that didn't go unnoticed by the other two men.

Ben pointed an index finger at his friend, his grin widening and Roman looked like he was going to be sick. Sinclair gave them both a look back and laughed heartily as he followed behind her, carrying food to the table.

SIX

Lights had been set up in each corner of the dining room to spotlight the baby grand piano. The room's ambiance felt different from the previous evening and Archer wasn't sure how she felt about it.

She'd changed into black slacks with a matching turtleneck. Her makeup was simple, except for the vibrant red lipstick that popped against her dark complexion.

Roman sat in Sinclair's office fielding telephone calls from the press and taking notes. Archer had taken the news of an alleged sex tape well, asking him to pass the last of the bacon in response. She hadn't responded at all when he told her about Paulo's impending nuptials, waving a dismissive hand as she'd risen from the table to clear away the dishes. Neither of them had known what to expect but they hadn't expected her to be so calm.

Sinclair had taken a few minutes after the meal to explain what would happen and what he wanted to discuss. Archer had listened intently, asking few questions and seeming agreeable with it all.

Now she looked toward him as he prepped the last of his notes. He, too, had changed and was wearing a white Polo shirt, khaki slacks, and a casual, navy blazer.

"You're most comfortable at the piano so I thought we'd start there," Sinclair said as he gestured for Archer to take a seat on the piano bench.

She tossed him a look then her gaze floated to Ben as he stood off to the side adjusting his camera. Archer sat, shifting against the wooden seat until she found a position that felt relaxed. She pulled her right leg up and rested her foot against her left thigh, her hands clutching her calf. She took a deep breath and then a second.

Sinclair sat down beside her and gave her a smile. "Forget Ben and forget the camera. You're having a conversation with me. It's just me and you. If anything bothers you or you're uncomfortable with any of my questions, just say so. We can stop whenever you need to."

He reached a hand out and squeezed her knee. His touch was warm and gentle and Archer closed her eyes for a moment, allowing herself to settle into the warmth of it. When she opened them, Sinclair trailed his fingers along the profile of her face and the gesture made her smile. "Are you ready?" he asked.

Archer nodded. "As ready as I'll ever be."

For some ninety-plus minutes Sinclair asked questions and Archer answered with an air of openness and honesty that few had ever gotten from her. With a slight of hand or a head tilt Sinclair directed Ben, gesturing when he wanted closeups of her face to catch a tear that rained from her eye, or the laughter that sometimes danced in the dark orbs.

She talked about her mother and their turbulent relationship; her relationship with Paulo Santana, and the scandal that was currently trending through social media. She shared her dreams for her future, where she felt she'd failed in the past and her short-term goals for the present. She wafted through a bevy of emotions; joy gleaming across her face one minute, sadness flooding her spirit the next. With expert precision Sinclair captured her vulnerability and her strength and even he was in awe of her expressiveness and the power she exuded even when the topic was hard. As he peeled away the many layers to Arch Santana he felt as if he were watching a butterfly being freed from its cocoon.

"So, do you see yourself marrying again?" he asked.

The slightest smiled pulled at her full lips and mirth danced deep in the look she gave him. "I never say never, but it will take an exceptional man to move me there. Do you know one?"

Sinclair smiled and gave her a slight shrug of his shoulders. He continued. "How about children? Do you look forward to being a mother yourself one day?"

There was a moment of pause as Archer pondered the question, looking as if she'd never given the thought any consideration.

"I honestly don't know," she finally answered. "The prospect scares me. I don't know if I'd be any good at it and I wouldn't want to make the same mistakes that my mother made." She paused again, taking a deep breath before she continued. "I think if the right man came along, I would probably jump at the opportunity to parent a child with him. And if that ever happens, what I do know for sure is that I will probably let my career go. I can't imagine being a mother and not devoting one-hundred percent of myself. I couldn't tour or spend days in the studio when I needed to be home with my babies."

Sinclair smiled. "So, you'd actually be a stay-at-home mother? Won't you miss the music?"

Archer smiled back. "There will always be music," she said as her hands suddenly skated across the piano keys, a warm tune floating between them. "Any child of mine will always have my music."

Archer had grown weary with Roman and his badgering. They had finished shooting hours earlier. Ben had bid them all farewell, needing to get to the airport for a flight and Sinclair had disappeared into his studio to play with the video they'd recorded. Roman had used their time alone to talk business. Although she held the man in high regard, more times than not he lectured her like he was her father and not her manager. She blew an audible gasp as she blinked her thick lashes at him.

"No!" she snapped. "I am not making a joint statement about our marriage ending amicably. I'm not going to let Paulo look like he's a good guy in all this. The son-of-a-bitch slept with my mother! My *mother*! In *our* goddamn bed! So, fuck him, his joint statement, his precious image, and fuck you for even making the damn suggestion," she shouted, her voice rising a few octaves. "The answer is *hell no*!"

Roman took his own deep breath. One hand waved up and down as if he were petting someone's dog. "Calm down, Archer. Please! This is about how you look, not Paulo."

She was still shouting. "I don't care anymore, Roman. I don't care if I look like a raving lunatic. If I make any statement it will be to tell Paulo to go straight to hell for all I care! He can go..."

"I got it!" Roman said, interrupting her rant. "We will pass on the joint statement, but the public, your fans, they're going to want to hear something from you."

"Tell the public to bite me!" she quipped.

Roman shook his head. "Let's just table the statement discussion for now. I didn't mean to upset you."

Archer changed the subject. "I've left three messages for my attorney. He called, and I've been trying to catch up with him. Have you heard from him? I need an update on my damn divorce!"

"I did. He called to say Paulo signed the paperwork and didn't contest any of your demands. He didn't make any claims for property or alimony. He also wanted you to know that he did file in Reno since the home Paulo has there fulfills the residency requirements. So, once the judge signs it'll be all over."

"How soon will that be? We started this process two months ago!"

"He said five, maybe six more days max."

"Good," she said. "The sooner the better. I want this to be finished."

Roman nodded. "You need to take a few days, Arch, before you head to New York to start the album. If you want, I can give you a ride back to Cambria, maybe arrange for you to spend some time at that spa you like before you head to the city."

"I'm not going to New York."

"Excuse me?"

"I'm going to work on my album here. "

"Here?"

"I'm staying here. With Sin."

Roman suddenly looked like he'd been hit with a stun gun. Perspiration beaded his brow and he was gulping air like a fish out of water as he processed her statement. "Archer, I don't think that's a good idea," he finally said.

"I guess it's a good thing I don't pay you to think about what's good for my personal life," she said. Giving the man one last look, she rose from her seat and stomped out the room.

Archer found Sinclair outside, swinging a large axe. He was splitting a downed tree into usable fire wood. Despite the cool temperatures he was bare-chested, his muscles bulging. Clearly, the chore was one he was accustomed to, his proficiency evident with each swing. As he lifted the axe above his head and slammed it down hard against the rounds of the tree trunk, his skin pulled tight, like black satin stretching over solid marble. It was a beautiful sight to behold.

Archer stood staring, the view taking her breath away. Suddenly she was having second thoughts about wanting to stay and insinuating herself into his life. Thinking that maybe Roman was right about it not being a good idea.

Sinclair turned, spying her out of the corner of his eye. She stood with her arms crossed tightly over her chest. Her expression was strained, her brow furrowed. Something was on her mind, clearly wreaking havoc with her spirit. She suddenly looked up, meeting his stare.

"What's wrong, Arch?"

She hesitated, her eyes shifting back and forth as she gathered her thoughts.

When she finally spoke, there was an air of desperation and longing in her tone that he had not heard before. "Can I stay here for awhile? With you? Please?" Her eyes widened as she met his gaze a second time.

"Yeah!" he said, with no hesitation. "Baby, you're welcome to stay here for as long as you need."

A slow smile pulled at her mouth and a hint of saline misted Archer's gaze. She nodded her gratitude and turned, heading back inside. At the door, she paused, taking a quick glance back over her shoulder. Without skipping a beat Sinclair had gone back to swinging his axe and she watched him intently, musing over the fact that he had twice called her *baby.*

Archer was singing, her sweet voice loud and clear as it echoed through the home. She would sing, play piano, sing some more and then go quiet, writing feverishly in that notebook of hers.

Sinclair had looked in on her a few times and each time she'd simply given him a smile before turning her focus back to her work in progress.

Roman had pulled out of the driveway an hour earlier, clearly unhappy with the two of them. So much so that Sinclair wasn't at all surprised when his cell phone rang; his sister calling.

"Hello, Kendra!"

"Why are you and my husband fighting?"

"I am not fighting with your husband. We just had a difference of opinion."

"So, what's going on with you and that woman?"

"What did your husband tell you?"

"Roman just said he was concerned."

"I know your husband better than that. I'm sure he had much more than that to say."

"Do you love her?"

Sinclair chuckled softly. "I'm getting to know her. We're just friends."

"But you're letting her move in with you?"

"Archer is not moving in, Kendra. She just needs a place to rest her heart for a moment."

His sister paused as she reflected on his comment. When she spoke, her voice was filled with concern. "Please, don't be that rebound guy, Sinclair. You deserve better than that, little brother."

"I love you, too, Kendra. And tell Roman not to worry. Archer is going to be fine. I'm going to be fine. Everyone is going to be fine."

Sinclair could feel his sister nodding her head into her receiver before she responded. "Mom says she may come visit. To see what's going on for herself."

"You talked to mom? Isn't she in Paris for a concert?"

"She is but she's planning on being back later this week."

"And you thought telling her about Archer was a good idea?"

"I didn't tell her. Roman did. I stopped her from cancelling her tour because she was ready to get on a plane to be on your doorstep tomorrow."

"Well, I appreciate that and thanks for the heads up."

"That's what big sisters are for, little brother!"

"I need to run. I'll call you in a few days."

"Promise?"

"I promise. And if I don't call you, I'm pretty sure you'll call me."

"Yes, I will. And Sinclair..." She took a deep breath.

"Yes?"

"Don't forget birth control, please! If you get that woman pregnant before you marry her, mommy will kill you!".

"Really, Kendra? You just had to go there?"

His sister laughed. "I love you, Sin!"

"I love you, too!"

Shaking his head Sinclair disconnected the call. More than ever he appreciated his family, despite their frequent annoyances. There was much love between them and as he learned more and more about Archer, it served to reinforce the joy his family brought to his own life.

"I owe Roman an apology," Archer said, the statement coming out of the blue.

Sinclair looked up from the paperwork he was reviewing. Video storyboards were strewn across the coffee table, couch, and floor. Archer was standing at the stove, stirring something that simmered in a pot. She was looking in his direction, waiting for him to respond.

He nodded. "Probably."

"No, definitely. I was rude to him."

"You do tend to be snarky when you get mad."

She blew a soft sigh. "I'm tired of being sad, Sin. And being angry all the time has completely exhausted me. I would really like to have an extended period of happy. I think I deserve it," she said as she turned her attention back to the food cooking on the stovetop.

Sinclair rose from his seat and moved to her side. She cut a quick eye in his direction as she cut off a burner and moved the pot to the center of the stove.

He pressed a large hand to the small of her back, his fingers gently kneading the skin beneath her tank top. His touch was heated and just shy of being intoxicating. Archer imagined that she could grow quite comfortable with Sinclair Cooper touching her on a regular basis. It was suddenly a challenge to focus. She took a breath as he spoke.

"Arch, I think you should talk to someone. A professional."

She bristled, the comment unexpected. She took a step to the side, disconnecting her body from his fingertips. "I don't need a shrink, Sin. I just need people to leave me alone."

"You need to talk to someone skilled to help you handle your anxiety and frustration. Someone who has an expertise in dealing with depression. Hiding out here with me isn't going to make things better overnight and your mental health isn't something to play with."

"You're afraid I'm going to try to hurt myself. I told you that was an accident."

"I'm afraid that you're never going to get off this roller coaster you've been riding. You want to be happy and that has to start with you healing whatever is hurting you."

A tear rolled down Archer's cheek and she swiped it away with the back of her hand. She changed the subject.

"Dinner's just about finished. Are you ready to eat?"

He nodded, his full lips lifting into the faintest smile. "It smells really good," he said, allowing the conversation to shift. Sinclair knew Archer needed time to reflect on his suggestion and he was willing to give her as much time as she needed. "What are we eating?" he asked.

"Grilled steak with roasted onions stuffed with blue cheese and bacon, glazed carrots, and mashed potatoes and gravy."

"If I didn't know better I'd swear you were trying to spoil me."

Archer grinned. "Goes to show you don't know much of anything at all!" she responded.

SEVEN

Archer leaned over the kitchen counter. She'd found some Ben & Jerry's Phish Food ice cream tucked away in the back of the big freezer in the garage. A large spoon was her new best friend and when Sinclair found her standing there in the kitchen, she'd already consumed half of the container.

She'd been pondering his suggestion, thinking about what he had said since he had said it. After dinner he had gone back to his papers and she had headed to the piano. They had tried to focus on their work, but had been intent on each other, stealing glances when they thought the other wasn't looking.

Archer knew Sinclair was right. For too many years she had been self-medicating her mood swings and bouts of depression with a too fast lifestyle, prescription meds, and work. Things weren't going to get any better if she didn't change how she chose to deal with her issues.

But she wasn't sure she was ready to take that step. She wasn't prepared to open herself in a way that exposed her darkest secrets. She just didn't want to face the demons she feared most.

She pulled another spoonful of ice cream into her mouth, slowly savoring the sweetness of chilled chocolate, gooey marshmallow and caramel swirls, and fudge shaped like little fish.

Sinclair watched her from the doorway. Archer stood with her back to him as she rested her elbows against the marble-topped island. She was wearing a long tee shirt that had risen up and over her backside, exposing her lush curves. Her rear end looked like nicely sized melons, full and ripe. At first glance he thought she was naked, but realized she was wearing a G-string that was lost in the crevice of her ass cheeks. As he stared, perverse thoughts clouded his mind and it took every ounce of fortitude he possessed to contain a rising erection that begged for attention.

The floor boards creaked as he shifted his weight from one foot to the other, hoping to ease the tightness out of the muscles below his waist. Archer turned, slightly surprised to find him standing there.

"Hey, what are you doing up?" she asked.

He smiled. "I should be asking you that. You haven't been to sleep at all, have you?"

Archer shook her head. "I don't sleep much."

"You need your rest, Arch."

"Too much on my mind."

He moved to the counter beside her. He dropped his hand against the back of hers, her fingers still clutching tightly to that spoon. He scooped ice cream and lifted her hand and the spoon to his mouth, sliding the cold mixture into his mouth. He hummed his appreciation.

"Hmm! That's good."

"Ice cream makes everything feel okay, even when it isn't."

She fed him another mouthful, took one last taste for herself, then dropped the spoon to the counter. She placed the lid back on the container and the container back into the freezer.

Sinclair was watching her intently. When she turned back toward him their gazes locked and held. He suddenly found himself holding his breath, air lost deep in his chest.

Arch bit down against her bottom lip, a wave of heat sweeping like a summer storm through her. She inhaled swiftly to stall the rise in her temperature. Her voice was a loud whisper when she finally spoke. "So, don't take this the wrong way, Sin, but every time we're near each other, I can't help but wonder if you're any good in bed!"

Sinclair laughed, but his expression was a tad tense. "Well, now that you've brought it up, you really make it hard on a brother!"

She eased herself slowly toward him. As she stepped against him he wrapped his arms around her and pulled her close. Archer closed her eyes and laid her head against his chest, reveling in the sensation of being in his arms.

"So, make love to me, Sin! I really want you to take me bed and make love to me."

Sinclair pressed a damp kiss to her forehead and allowed his lips to linger there. When he pulled himself from her his tone was calm and soothing as he turned her down.

"We can't, Arch. You know we can't. Not while you're going through what you're going through. You're not in a good place and sex isn't what you need right now."

Archer slid a hand between them, her manicured nails lightly grazing the length of his manhood. "Sex is exactly what I need," she said, as she eased a hand past the elastic of his sleeping pants and wrapped her palm around his dick. "Nothing serious," she murmured. "Just a casual fuck between friends."

Sinclair felt himself swell magnificently, his male anatomy fully engorged as she stroked him boldly. His flesh tightened and stretched in every direction fathomable. He jumped, her unexpected touch firing nerve endings he didn't even know he had. His heartbeat was racing, and perspiration suddenly beaded across his brow. He scooted his hips backward as he grabbed her wrist to stall her ministrations.

He shook his head. "Stop, Archer. Please, don't do that!"

Archer blew a soft sigh as she released the hold she had on his person. She slid her hand from his pants and pressed her palm to his chest, strumming her fingers against his tee shirt.

"I get it," she said, feigning indifference. "I wouldn't want me either."

He shook his head vehemently. "Baby, it doesn't have anything to do with wanting you. Because I want you. I want you so badly it hurts. And if we cross that line there will be nothing casual about it. Because I don't *casually fuck* women I care about."

He paused, seeming to gather his thoughts as he struggled with what his body was doing. "This is about doing what's right. And right now, I need to take the lead because you're not in the headspace to make that kind of decision."

"So, you're going to make it for me?"

"Damn right I am, Arch. And the next time we're in this position I hope you'll be able to make that decision for yourself."

"I might turn you down then," she said, a hint of attitude in her voice.

A sly smile lifted his lips. He took a step forward as he eased an arm slowly around her waist and pulled her back to him. "You won't," Sinclair said.

Archer inhaled swiftly, the searing gaze he was giving her suddenly sending her into a slow spin. "Any chance I can change your mind?" she asked, biting down against her bottom lip. She slowly rotated her pelvis against the rise of nature that still pressed eagerly against the front of his cotton pants.

Sinclair chuckled softly. He leaned and pressed a kiss to Archer's cheek, his other hand gently cupping the side of her face. Then just like that he eased himself from her and exited the room.

Archer stood like stone until she heard him enter his room and close the door. She took a deep breath, and then another, and then she moved back to the freezer to finish what was left of the ice cream.

Sinclair leaned his back against the door, his hands lost down his pants as he stroked the tension out of his dick. Walking away from Archer probably had to be the hardest thing he'd had to do in a very long time. Because he hadn't wanted to walk away. If he were honest he had wanted to take her right there, on the kitchen counter and make her his. He couldn't begin to fathom how she could think he wouldn't want her.

He thought about the warmth of her palm and the feel of her fingers as she had stroked him. Her touch had been heated and teasing. Just thinking back to the memory had his pulse surging and every muscle in his body quivering.

He held his breath as he strained against the sensations sweeping from his groin to his midsection, heat flooding through his body. He took deep breaths to calm his nerves and then he headed toward the bathroom for a cold shower.

Sinclair was up early. He hadn't gotten much sleep, tossing and turning most of the night. He found himself second guessing whether he'd done the right thing. Wondering if he should have kept how he felt about Archer to himself. Questioning why his desire for her was feeling more like a need, intense and urgent.

He had kissed her cheek because there would have been no turning back if he had kissed her lips. But he had been desperate to kiss her lips, imagining how soft and luscious her mouth would be against his own. The nearness of her had ignited fire in his bloodstream and the sanguine flow still simmered through his veins. Archer had gotten under his skin and she lingered there like a virus that could not be contained.

But from their first encounter he had recognized the desperation tainting her spirit. The hurt and loneliness was all too familiar. He'd understood her manic moments and the too frequent outbursts she justified as too much stress. He had seen it all before and he knew she could be helped. He knew how things could change for the better and Archer could find the peace and happiness she desperately yearned for.

He also knew that to cross the boundaries of their friendship would only muddy the waters as she did the necessary work to heal.

His mother was listening intently as he explained everything he'd been rationalizing for most of the night. When he finished, Roberta Cooper blew a soft. A wave of silence billowed between through the cell phone line. When the matriarch finally spoke, her soft voice was thick with concern.

"You can't save everyone, Sinclair. I know you want to be her super hero, but this is something she's going to have to do for herself."

"I get that, Mom. And, I believe Archer is ready. She just needs someone to hold her hand as she takes that first step."

"You do know there's going to come a point, that if it all goes well, where she's going to let your hand go, right?"

"Of course, and I know just how beautiful that can be. I know firsthand how Archer will be able to blossom and I want that for her. I want it for her like I wanted it for you. It's why I knew you'd understand."

"I do understand. But I also know you care more about this young woman than you're admitting."

"I do care about her. I've been totally open about that."

"It's more than that. I think you've fallen in love with Archer Santana and if that's true you need to be prepared in case she doesn't love you back."

Sinclair didn't bother to respond. There was no point in arguing or denying the comment. His mother knew him better than anyone else, so he didn't need to.

"Thanks, Mom," he said softly, no other words necessary.

"I will always be here to support you, Sinclair. You know that."

"I do."

"How long are you planning to be gone?"

"Just a few days. I'll be back before you have to leave for Italy."

"Good. We'll talk more, I'm sure."

When Archer entered the kitchen, Sinclair had his head in the refrigerator, debating French yogurt or leftover chicken casserole for breakfast. For the briefest moment things between them felt awkward and then just like that they didn't. The two slipped easily into the comfort zone they'd found with each other.

"What are you all dressed up for?" she asked, noting his suit and tie and the overnight bag that rested at the front door.

"I need to be in LA for a few days. I have an appointment with the studio executives this afternoon. If you need anything just call my office if you can't reach me."

"When are you coming back?"

"I'll only be gone for a few days."

"And it's still okay for me to stay here?"

"Of course! I said you could stay as long as you needed, and I meant that."

Archer moved to Sinclair's side, leaning to peer into the refrigerator with him. "Can I give you a hand?"

"I was trying to decide what I wanted to eat."

"How about I make you a Western omelet?"

"I don't want to put you through any trouble."

"It's no trouble, Sin," she said as she reached for the eggs. "It's the least I can do to repay your hospitality."

Sinclair gave her a bright smile. "If you insist..."

She smiled back. "So, how'd you sleep last night?" she asked as she pulled, cheese and vegetables from the refrigerator drawer and began to prepare breakfast.

"Probably about as well as you did."

"I'm sorry for that. I really didn't mean to make things uncomfortable for you."

"You didn't. You only spoke what we've both been thinking."

She nodded as he watched her crack eggs into a bowl, seasoning them with salt and pepper before pouring the mixture into a small fry pan. After laying cheese, onions, green peppers, tomato and chunks of ham down the center of the eggs, she folded the rising omelet and flipped it to cook on the other side.

Sinclair moved to the cabinets and pulled down two plates. After setting them on the counter he turned to make a pot of hot coffee. Minutes later the duo was sitting across from each other at the kitchen table enjoying their meal.

"Arch, may I ask you a question?"

She looked up from her plate, her head bobbing. "Of course! You can ask me anything."

Sinclair rested his fork against his empty plate. "Why would you think I wouldn't want you?"

She lifted her eyes to his, struck by the intensity of the look he was giving her. His question threw her, and it took a moment to give him an answer.

"Because I'm broken, Sin. I'm broken, and I don't know if I can be fixed. Why would you want that in your life?"

He nodded. "You are incredibly special, Archer. You are a gift to this world and you have been a gift to me. I've enjoyed getting to know you. Flaws and all! But I don't see a broken woman. What I see is a woman who has spent her entire life pretending to be something she's not. A woman who just wants to be herself. Who is trying to figure out who she is and not who everyone else says she is. You've been under a spotlight since you were eight-years old, with perfect strangers thinking they had the right to judge everything you said and did and now you're reclaiming your time."

Archer gave him a smile. "You have been very kind to me. Not many people have been kind."

"You need to start surrounding yourself with better people."

"I have a long list of things I need to start doing," she said, slipping into thought.

Sinclair watched her as a blanket of quiet slipped between them. "I hate to eat and run, but I need to get on the road," he said finally. He stole a glance at his wrist watch. "Are you going to be okay by yourself?"

She gave him another smile. "I'll be fine. I'm going to work on my music, hopefully write a few more songs and I'll be right here when you get back."

Sinclair rose from his seat, lifting his plate and coffee cup to the sink.

Archer called his name.

"Yes?"

"I no longer have doubts. I'm pretty sure you're probably really good in bed."

Sinclair laughed. "You actually had doubts?"

She looked at him with a raised brow, mischief shimmering in her dark eyes. "I was definitely curious!"

And what brought you to the conclusion that I probably am good?"

Archer swept past him with her own dirty dishes that she dropped into the kitchen sink.

"You've been blessed!" she said as she gave him a wink of her eye. She moved past him in the opposite direction. "Immensely blessed!" she exclaimed as she tapped her palm against his backside.

EIGHT

For the first few hours Archer found the quiet only slightly disconcerting. There was something about being in an empty house, in the woods, alone, that felt slightly off-putting. But she didn't feel unsafe, and for the first time in a long time, alone didn't feel lonely.

After checking that all the doors were locked she peered out the windows. In the distance, a herd of deer stood grazing at the edge of the manicured lawn. The outside landscape was a forest of tall trees and a green canopy of lush leaves. The last threads of the afternoon sun shimmered through the tree line and all of it felt like a scene out of someone else's storybook.

Mesmerized, she watched the deer for a good few minutes before returning to the piano and a song that was spinning in her head.

Archer loved the music. Everything about the simple words that became complex melodies and the notes that spun into full-fledged compositions brought her immense joy. She was happiest when she was singing, small venues and intimate supper clubs her favorite places to perform. The creative process was everything to her and it felt like it had been forever since the words and the notes flowed like water from a faucet.

She had a vision for her next album, one that went against the grain of what her record label was expecting. She was determined that this album would be art, fueled by her emotions and the wealth of talent she brought to her craft. No one else's idea of who she was, or what they thought she believed, would see the light of day in any song she planned for this musical collection. There would be no collaborations, no other writers, no one else's noise clouding her heart. Every ounce of what would come would be all Archer.

Hours later Archer was lost in the music. Her hands were dancing across the keys, her eyes closed, the heavy syncopation of heartbreak spilling out into the room. She was a woman possessed, something no one would ever be able to explain guiding each, and every note.

She didn't hear the loud knock on the front door. Nor did she hear it open as someone let themselves inside. She was completely oblivious to the woman calling hello from the entrance. It was minutes later when she finally opened her eyes to find Roberta Cooper watching her, tears dampening the matriarch's cheeks.

The family resemblance was undeniable. Sinclair was the spitting image of his mother and Roberta Cooper was stunning. The many promotional photographs of her didn't begin to do her justice. She had blessed her son with her black licorice complexion. Her skin was blemish and makeup free. She epitomized the adage that black didn't crack, looking more like Sinclair's much older sister than his mother.

Archer came to an abrupt halt, her hands resting harshly against the piano keys. The clanging sound resonated through the air in greeting.

"I hope I didn't frighten you, dear," Roberta said, her thin lips lifting in a warm smile. "I knocked but you didn't hear so I let myself in." She waved a spare key as if to help explain her presence there. Her smiled widened.

"I wasn't expecting anyone," Archer managed to say, her eyes skating from side to side.

"I wasn't planning to come so soon, but my last performance was cancelled. Something to do with the ceiling caving in at the venue. So, I decided to come check on that son of mine. But I hear he's traveling for the next few days."

"He went to Los Angeles this morning. He said he'd be back before the end of the week."

Roberta nodded. She moved to the piano and took a seat on the bench beside Archer. "I'm Roberta Cooper. Sinclair's mother," she said as she wrapped Archer in a warm hug. "I'm excited to meet you, Archer. I'm a big fan."

Archer blushed as she hugged the woman back. "I'm the one who's a fan, Mrs. Cooper. I'm

---

actually having a fan girl moment right now and I'm trying not to let it show."

Roberta laughed. "Well, you and I will fangirl together. But, please, call me, Roberta. Mrs. Cooper was my husband's mother and I couldn't stand that woman!"

Archer laughed with her, her anxiety fading.

Roberta gave her another bright smile. "What were you playing? It was beautiful!"

"Thank you. I was just messing around," Archer said softly.

Roberta strummed her fingers down the keyboard and back. "I told my son this baby would come in handy. He was certain no one else would ever play it when I wasn't around. I'm glad you've proved him wrong."

Archer clasped her hands together in her lap, suddenly feeling like she might have imposed on his mother's personal space. Most musicians were possessive about their instruments. "I hope you don't mind…"

"Of course not! It's what it's here for!" Roberta quipped. The matriarch reached for Archer's notebook, reading the lines of music Archer had penned on the open page. She seemed to be processing the music in her head and then she rested the journal back on the music rack and began to play.

Archer closed her eyes, slightly surprised to hear what she had written being played by someone else. Roberta suddenly shifted the key and the dynamics of the song felt as if it had turned on a dime. Archer's eyes flew open, the surprise of it washing over her expression. She met the look Roberta was giving her.

"I'm still playing with the lyrics," Archer said, answering an unasked question. "Once I nail those I'll know what key it should be in."

Roberta nodded again. "Your vocal range is like what, four or five octaves?"

Archer shrugged her shoulders. "Something like that."

"You're blessed with an incredible instrument. I'm sure it'll be perfect in whatever key you sing it in."

"Thank you," Archer answered. "Are you hungry? I made a pan of baked spaghetti and there's salad fixings. There might be some leftover chicken casserole, too, if Sin didn't eat it all."

"I heard you're a marvelous cook. And I am hungry. I'd love to try your spaghetti."

"You heard...?"

"When I spoke to Sinclair he told me you've been keeping him well fed."

Archer wasn't sure how she felt about Sinclair discussing her with his mother. Her confliction showed on her face.

"My son is quite smitten with you," Roberta said, seeming to read her mind. "He thought this would be a good time for us to get to know each other without him being around to make you uncomfortable."

"He didn't say anything," Archer noted.

"Probably because my schedule was so uncertain. I'm sure he didn't want to make you nervous unnecessarily if I wasn't able to make it here." Roberta reached for her hand and squeezed it gently. "Why don't I go take my bags to my room and wash up while you fix me a plate. And I hope you'll join me. You haven't eaten already, have you?"

Archer shook her head. "No, ma'am."

"Great! I hate eating alone." Roberta moved onto her feet. She eased back across the room, turning around midway to give Archer another warm smile. "We're going to be great friends," she said. "I look forward to knowing you, Archer."

The two women were laughing hysterically as they washed and dried the few dirty dishes from their meal. Roberta leaned across the center island, a glass of red wine spinning between the palms of her hands.

"So, for three years I made him wear the same skunk costume for Halloween. He was just so darn cute in it! Then he turned six and insisted if he couldn't be a cowboy, he wasn't going to be anything at all."

"Was that a bad thing?"

"It is when your mother is obsessed with the holidays! I always made these elaborate costumes for him and his sister for Halloween. Christmas, I put up trees in every room in the house and we eat extravagant Thanksgiving dinners every day for a week. And don't get me started on Valentine's Day and the Fourth of July."

Archer leaned back against the counter and sipped her own glass of wine. "I don't think I've ever dressed up for Halloween," she said, trying to remember if they had ever celebrated anything when she'd been a little girl.

"Well, then this year will be your first. I always throw an elaborate Halloween open house for the neighborhood. Last year Sinclair came as RuPaul."

Archer laughed. "He still dresses up?"

"He balks and pretends he's too grown for it, but I'll bet he's already planning his next costume. He hates losing the Most Creative contest and his sister has taken the title from him for the last two years. Kendra and Roman were Minions last year and Oompa Loompas the year before that. They're crowd favorites every year, so you and Sinclair have your work cut out."

Archer laughed. She suddenly yawned, slapping her hand over her mouth, her eyes widening. "Excuse me," she said.

"It's contagious!" Roberta yawned with her. "I should probably call it a night. I'm actually exhausted."

"Thank you," Archer said. "I've really enjoyed talking to you."

"The pleasure has been all mine, Archer."

"Will my playing disturb you, Roberta? I'd like to work for a little longer if it won't be a problem."

"No, dear. It won't be a problem at all. Play to your heart's content! I would never turn down a free Archer Santana concert!"

It was almost daybreak when Archer finally retired to her bed. Satisfaction painted her spirit, everything feeling like she was headed in the right direction. She had finished her song and started on another and if she could have found an extra ounce of energy she would have kept going. But she was exhausted, and sleep was calling her loudly.

After stripping out of her clothes, she dropped naked into the bed and wrapped the bedclothes tightly around her lean frame. Her cell phone rested on the nightstand, the screen flagging dozens of missed calls and messages. There was only one call she was interested in and when she saw that he had tried calling her more than once, Archer sat upright in the bed and called him back. Sinclair answered on the first ring.

"Are you okay?"

"Sorry. I turned off the ringer on my phone and left it here in the bedroom. I didn't realize you were trying to check up on me. But I'm fine."

"My mother's not driving you crazy, is she?"

"I like your mother."

"I was trying to warn you she was coming. I didn't want you to be surprised and I didn't want you to leave."

"It's all good. We're having a great time together. I'm not planning on going anywhere before you get back."

There was a moment of pause as he seemed to breathe a sigh of relief. When he next spoke, his voice had dropped to a loud whisper.

"Don't tell anyone," Sinclair said, "but I think I actually miss you."

Archer giggled. "Well, I'm certain I miss you, Sin. I can't wait for you to hear what I've been working on."

"I have a few meetings tomorrow and then I'll be heading back. If you need me before then, for anything, you just call. Okay?"

"I will."

"Promise me, Arch. Anything!"

"I promise. You need to stop worrying."

"Not going to happen," he said with a soft chuckle.

Archer tried to contain the full grin that spread abundantly across her face. "Sweet dreams, Sin!"

"Sweet dreams, baby!"

Archer woke to the aroma of cinnamon and sugar wafting through the air. A pan of warm cinnamon rolls and a carafe of hot coffee rested on the kitchen island. There was a slow cooker on the counter and something inside was simmering slowly.

Roberta was seated in a window seat in the family room, her iPad resting on her lap as she sipped her own cup of coffee. The temperature had taken a slight dip, the threat of rain imminent and the matriarch was wrapped in an oversized blanket.

"Good morning!" she chimed cheerily.

Archer gave the woman a slight wave of her hand. "Good morning. It smells really good in here."

"Today felt like a comfort food kind of day. There's sausage and bacon in the oven to go with those cinnamon buns," she said, "and I'm making a wonderful chili and cheese soup for dinner. I'll whip up a pan of cornbread later to go with it."

"That sounds good," Archer answered as she poured herself a cup of coffee. "I think a peach dump cake would be perfect for dessert."

"I've never made dump cake. You'll have to show me your recipe."

Archer nodded and moved to the sofa. She settled down with her own blanket. "What are you reading?" she asked. She took a sip from her large coffee mug as she eyed the other woman curiously.

"It's a wonderful romance by an author named KM Jackson. She writes these delightful, humorous love stories. You should read one of her books one day. You won't be disappointed."

Archer took another sip of her coffee. She was embarrassed to say that it had been forever since she'd last read a book and she had never read a romance novel. From the expression on the older woman's face Archer was thinking that there was much she was missing out on."

They sat quietly together, Roberta reading and Archer toying with the lyrics to yet another song. Her writing was moving swiftly, emotion spilling into new songs with a ferocity that Archer hadn't expected. She had more material than she ever imagined having and she knew she was almost ready to go into the studio. Almost.

Conversation between the two was easy. Roberta liked to talk, and Archer enjoyed listening to the stories she shared. The woman made her feel comfortable, something endearing about her outlook on life. Her positive spirit was infectious and being in her presence made Archer feel better about everything.

Archer was back at the piano when Roberta eased into the room and sat down beside her. She closed her eyes as she listened to the gentle rhythm that danced out of the young woman's fingers. The song was an easy, gentle ballad, feeling almost like a lullaby.

"That's very pretty!" Roberta exclaimed.

"Thank you. I think it's going to be incredible with an orchestra of violins and flutes."

Roberta smiled. "Consider a single harpist for your intro. It lends itself to the subtlety of the tune, yet it makes a dynamic statement."

Archer pondered the suggestion, drifting into thought. As she did, Roberta nudged her with a slight tap against her hip. Archer scooted over to give the woman easier access to the keyboard. Roberta began to play, and Archer found herself grinning from ear to ear.

The woman was a master pianist renowned for her jazz improvisations. She had perfect pitch and was known to marry classical harmonization with easy jazz stylings. She'd recorded with some of the best in the industry. Her walls were lined with hundreds of gold and platinum records and she'd become the queen of the Grammy awards in her category. She was brilliant, and Archer was in awe of her talent.

She applauded eagerly when the song ended. "I wish I could play like that!"

"You do play like that. I've heard you play, remember. Don't shortchange yourself, Archer. You are exceptionally gifted!"

"I appreciate you saying that. I wrestle with self-doubt all the time."

"We all do. But you can't let that consume you. You're good and you need to own it."

"Sinclair says he doesn't play. I really found that hard to believe. The incomparable Roberta Cooper is his mother for crying out loud!"

"Sinclair told you right. Despite all my efforts I could not get that son of mine to play. He had no interest at all in the piano or any inclination for music. And my daughter Kendra just dabbled at it casually. She doesn't play very well either!"

Archer laughed heartily.

Roberta moved back onto her feet. "I should go mix up that cornbread and get it in the oven."

"Can I help?" Archer asked, rising with her. "We can do the peach dump cake while we're at it."

Minutes later the two women had prepped a pan of cornbread and Archer was sharing her dessert recipe. "It's actually too easy to be so good," she said.

"So, it's like a cobbler?"

"Very similar." Archer poured two large cans of sliced peaches and heavy syrup into a greased baking dish. She seasoned the peaches with a teaspoon of vanilla extract, a few shakes of cinnamon and a dash of nutmeg. She opened a box of yellow cake mix and sprinkled it over the peaches, using a spatula to smooth the cake mix out evenly. She dotted the top of the cake mix with two sticks of butter that she had sliced into pats. With the prep finished she slid the pan into a three-hundred-fifty-degree oven to bake for a half-hour until the top was golden and crunchy.

"Voila!" she exclaimed with a flourish of her dish towel. "Easy peasy! When it's done we serve it with ice cream and that's all there is to it."

"I'm going to like this dessert," Roberta said, as she leaned to peer inside the oven. "Something tells me I'm going to like this a lot!"

Archer moved to fill two glasses with wine. She passed one to her new friend and the two women both leaned across the center island.

"May I ask you something?" Archer questioned as she twisted the crystal goblet between her fingers.

"Anything."

"How did you manage to have your career and your family and not lose your mind?"

Roberta smiled. "Oh, I lost my mind!" she exclaimed. She gestured for Archer to follow as she moved to the living room to take a seat. "My son hasn't told you what it was like to grow up with his crazy mother?"

"He doesn't like to talk about himself."

Roberta nodded. "Neither of my children talk about it, but I put them through hell. It was a few rough years for all of us. I was being pulled in more directions than I cared to count, and it took its toll. My music suffered, my marriage was hanging on by a thread, and my children endured hardships no child should ever be made to bear. I was a complete and total wreck and for a while there I wasn't sure I was going to make it out alive on the other side. "

The woman sighed and gulped a large sip of her beverage. "I'm sure I don't have to tell you what this business will do to you if you let it. Trying to please people who truly don't care about you. Wanting to keep your fans happy. Struggling to satisfy the label's demands. If you let it, the music industry will swallow you whole, spit you out and leave you broken.

"I got lost in a vicious cycle. I was popping uppers to keep me going, downers so I could relax and a host of other drugs just to try and maintain my sanity. It all came crashing down when I tried to drown my sixteen-year-old son because he wouldn't go buy me pot so I could relax. "

Archer's eyes widened, her mouth falling open in shock. "You tried to drown Sinclair?"

Tears clouded Roberta's gaze. "It was not the first time I had abused my son. Or my daughter for that matter. But I own every vile thing I ever did to either of them. I thank God, every day that they were able to forgive me and that we have the relationships that we have today. But it took all of us years of therapy to get to this point."

Archer shifted forward in her seat. "How did you..."

"How did I save myself?"

Archer nodded. "Yes."

"I did what you're doing now. I stepped back, took an accounting of everything that was wrong and pushed reset. I eliminated whatever was toxic; people, bad habits, everything! Then I took back control."

"And it was that easy?"

Roberta gave Archer a look. Her eyes still glistened, her tears misting the dark orbs. "No, it was hard as hell. Probably one of the hardest things I've ever had to do. But I didn't pretend I could do it alone. Someone who loved me extended a helping hand, and I took it."

"Someone?"

"Sinclair's father. That man is pure gold. He should have walked away and if he had, I couldn't have blamed him. But he hung in there with me. He tossed me a life line and he wouldn't allow me to let go. He loved me when I was at my worse and he loved me through my lowest moments and because he loved me, I can sit here and tell you that I not only survived, but I thrived. More importantly, I learned how to love myself and I discovered that I was worthy of being loved."

"You were lucky. You had your husband and your children. You had something to fight for and

I'm sure that made all the difference. I don't have anything."

Roberta shook her head. "That's not true. You have yourself, Archer. And you, Archer Santana, are worth fighting for. I didn't do what I did for anyone but myself. Even with all the bad shit that I did to my kids they loved me and because I was their mother they would have continued to love me whether I worked to get better or not. But they wouldn't have liked me, and they wouldn't have accepted my bad choices or continued to let me be in their lives. All their sentences would have started with 'I love my mother, but...' So, I couldn't let it be about them. It had to be about my needs and what I wanted for my life. And I wanted more. Doing the work definitely made me a better parent, but I did it, so I could be a better person."

"And now?"

"The work never ends. I will forever need to do a twelve-step program to battle my addictions and I stay in therapy to for my mental health. But I can honestly say that the breadth and depth of my self-awareness is light years from where it had been years ago."

Archer sat back against the sofa cushions, taking it all in. For a moment, neither spoke.

"I need help," Archer suddenly muttered. "I need help and I don't know where to start. Where do I start?" Tears were raining down her face.

Roberta moved to Archer's side and wrapped her arms around the young woman's shoulders. "You've already taken the hardest step. You asked for help. The rest is all downhill from here. I would like to help you, Archer, if you'll let me."

Archer swiped at her eyes. She was about to protest, but the look Roberta was giving her stalled the objections perched on the tip of her tongue. Instead, Archer nodded her head in appreciation.

Roberta smiled. "I have a really good friend I'd like to introduce you to. She helped save my life and I know she can do the same for you. She'll point you where you need to go. If I have your permission, I'll give her a call and ask her to come meet with you."

"Thank you," Archer said.

Roberta hugged her warmly. "You and I have to stick together if we have any hope of keeping Sinclair in line! By the way," Archer laughed, "what are your intentions with my son?"

Archer laughed. "My intentions?"

"I didn't stutter. I hear how you two talk about each other. Both of you get all giggly and silly. I know young love when I see it!"

Archer blushed, her eyes widening. She sputtered. "We...I...it's..."

Roberta chuckled. "It's okay. Both of you have plenty of time to explore whatever is developing between you. For now, take the time you need for you. Mother's intuition tells me

Sinclair's not going anywhere. He'll be right here when you're ready."

Before Archer could reply the front door swung open and Sinclair announced his return, calling both of their names from the entranceway. As if they'd somehow managed to talk him up, the two women gave each other a look and burst out laughing.

Sinclair moved into the room. His gaze swept from one to the other. His smile was canyon-wide.

NINE

"I like when you smile," Sinclair said. "You have a beautiful smile. You really should do it more often."

Archer laughed. "You have to admit, Sin, I haven't had much to smile about lately."

The two sat together on the family room sofa, sharing a blanket. She rested against his chest, legs extended as they held hands. She took pleasure in twisting her fingers between his, palms kissing sweetly as they teased each other gently.

A fire burned in the fire place, the crackle of heat filling the room nicely. Dinner had been a reunion of sorts, as he had caught her and his mother up on all he'd accomplished in Los Angeles, even sharing a few snippets from the documentary about Archer. After dessert, each of them consuming second helpings of the dump cake and ice cream, they'd played Sequence, a board game that was a family favorite. Sinclair had enjoyed teaching her the intricacies of the game. After Roberta had beat them both, twice, she had retired to her room, allowing them some privacy.

Sinclair reached out and drew a hand down the side of her face, his fingers gently caressing her profile. "So, what have you and my mother been up to since she got here?"

Archer shrugged. "Mostly we talked."

"She does do that," Sinclair said. "Sometimes it's hard to get a word in with her."

Archer smiled. "And we cooked together. Tomorrow she's going to teach me your favorite macaroni and cheese recipe. "

"My mother must really like you. Usually she hates having anyone else in the kitchen with her. And she *never* shares her recipes! I don't even think my sister knows that recipe."

"I have that effect on people," Archer said.

He nodded, pausing as he stared at her. "I guess she told you that she tried to kill me."

Archer lifted her gaze to his as he eyed her for a reaction. She nodded. "I wasn't sure how to take that."

"It's all water under the bridge. We had some stuff to work through and we did. I understand it was about her disease and not about her truly wanting to hurt me. I know my mother loves me."

"She really does. She said you did counseling, too?"

"When your mother tries to drown you, it requires a lot of therapy to get over. We also did family therapy with my father and sister, and my mother and I did therapy together."

"I didn't think black people did therapy."

Sinclair laughed. "Historically, as a people, we did therapy on Sunday afternoons, at the family dinner table. Everyone said their piece and then went their separate ways. You didn't talk about your problems with outsiders and heaven forbid you tell a family secret to a stranger. Old people believed in keeping their family dirt secret!"

"That was every day in my house with my mother."

He nodded. "Therapy is sometimes necessary and there is nothing wrong with seeking professional help. Sometimes medication is necessary to help with depression and anxiety and that's okay, too. You need to do whatever it takes to make yourself better, so you can live a happy and productive life."

Archer sat with that message for a few minutes, taking it all in as Sinclair addressed some of her concerns. He'd had his own fears and readily shared what had motivated him to trust the process.

Time ticked by too quickly. They sat talking for hours, oblivious to everything around them. Archer felt comfortable sharing things she had never shared with anyone before and Sinclair listened, genuinely interested in what she had to say. They laughed, flirted unabashedly, and enjoyed their time together. They had missed each other and readily admitted it. Before either realized how much time had passed, the sun was beginning to rise in the distance. The faintest rays of light were starting to peek through the windows.

"I can't believe we've been up all night," Sinclair said. "You're a bad influence on me Archer Santana."

Archer laughed. "Don't get it twisted, Sinclair Cooper! I'm the best thing that's ever happened to you."

Sinclair's gaze danced with hers, a two-step that had the room spinning in surreal motion. Everything in that moment told him she had never spoken truer words.

There was a wave of energy that swept between them that neither had the words to describe. It was as if a current of electricity had been tinged with honey, the sweetness of it slapping them both broadside. Everything suddenly felt right; as near to perfect as either could have ever imagined.

Archer moved to her feet, anxiety suddenly threatening her moment of feel good. Sinclair eyed her curiously as she stood twisting her hands together nervously.

He stood with her, pulling her into his arms as he wrapped his arms tightly around her torso. "Talk to me," he said softly, the words a gentle whisper of warm breath against her ear.

She nodded her head vehemently, searching for the words to ask what was suddenly on her mind. She was nervous, and Archer had never felt like that with any man. But she hadn't cared about any other man the way she found herself caring for Sinclair.

"It's okay," he said, gently urging her to share whatever was on her heart. "You know you can tell me anything, right?"

Archer took a deep breath, and then a second before she ventured to speak. She took a step back, needing to put a hint of distance between their two bodies. Then she asked the question that had been on her mind.

"What's next for us, Sin? What's going to happen after you finish your documentary and you get tired of me being in your space and I have to go back home?"

"What do you want to happen?" he asked as he moved back against her, pulling her back into his arms. He gently stroked her back. "What does Arch want?"

Archer hesitated. "Honest?"

"I don't want you to lie to me! I thought we had already established that?"

She nodded and then she answered. "I want the fairy tale and the happy ending. I want you to be my Prince Charming. I want you to love me. Even the me that can sometimes be very unlikeable. I want it all, Sin!"

Amusement painted Sinclair's expression. He pulled her even closer, tightening the hold he had on her torso. He pressed his cheek to her cheek, the warmth of her skin gently caressing his own.

He held her and then without an ounce of hesitation, Sinclair kissed her.

When Sinclair captured her mouth with his, Archer felt her heart stop, reset, and then start again. She'd had her share of first kisses before, but Sinclair kissing her was like every spectacular holiday rolled into the surprise party of all surprise parties! Fireworks exploded, confetti dropped, and the sounds of a marching band celebrated the moment.

He kissed her, and kept kissing her, latching onto her lips as if he never intended to let go. He was every one of Archer's dreams come true and she knew no one else could ever kiss her like that and come close to making her feel the way Sinclair Cooper was making her feel.

He tasted like mint and peaches. His tongue teased hers, boldly exploring the warm cavity as he played with her sensibilities. She clutched the front of his shirt, leaning her weight against him. His mouth glided against hers, moving with an ease and grace that claimed her heart and soul.

A loud cough echoed from the doorway, interrupting the moment. "Good morning!" Sinclair's mother chimed cheerily. "Looks like you two have had a productive night."

Sinclair took a step back, finally releasing the hold he had on Archer. He pressed his forehead to hers, his eyes closed, his breathing labored. He took a deep breath and held it, finally opening his eyes to stare into hers. Archer's mouth curled in the sweetest smile and then she laughed. He couldn't help but laugh with her.

"Good morning!" they replied simultaneously.

Roberta shook her head. "Did you two get any sleep? Or have you spent the entire night sucking face?"

Sinclair rolled his eyes skyward. "Only my mother," he said, as Archer laughed again.

"I thought I'd make pancakes for breakfast," Roberta said, moving toward the kitchen. "Are you two ready for something to eat?"

"I'm not hungry," Sinclair said, fighting to suppress a yawn. "I'm actually tired. His comment was directed at his mother, although his gaze never left Archer's face.

"I'm feeling energized," Archer said. "In fact, I think I'm ready to do some work."

"Well, I'm not. I think I'm going to go get a shower and grab a quick nap." Sinclair pressed his mouth to hers, giving her a quick kiss.

Archer smiled as she extended her arms over her head and stretched her lithe frame up and out. "I have a love song to write," she said. "I'll nap later!"

The home's doorbell ringing pulled Archer from the trance she'd fallen into. The morning had flown by, leaving her behind as she'd pounded out cords and struggled with transitions.

Twice, Roberta had commented, suggesting a shift from one key to another and then a change in syncopation for the chorus. The rest of the time the older woman had gone about her business as she'd enjoyed the beauty of the music. Sinclair had disappeared behind his closed door and both women had ignored him, unconcerned with what he might have been doing.

It was when the doorbell rang that he suddenly reappeared, showered and changed, looking like new money on a good banking day.

Completely lost in what she'd been doing, Archer felt like she had to reacclimate herself to her surroundings and she realized she was only feeling out of sorts because she was exhausted. As if reading her mind, Roberta entered the room with a cup of hot coffee in hand.

"You look like you need this," the matriarch said as she gently patted Archer on the back.

Archer nodded. "Thank you."

Both women looked up as Sinclair entered the room accompanied by a woman he seemed to know well. The two were chatting warmly, the casual conversation about what he'd been doing since the last time they'd talked. His friend's midwestern accent was thick and distinctive as she asked questions to catch herself up with his doings. She reminded Archer of the game show maven who'd made a fortune turning letters in full-length designer gowns. She was fair-skinned with hair the color of corn silk. She wore a sharply tailored navy-blue suit and a spectacular pair of high heels.

Archer stood as the stranger and Roberta greeted each other warmly. The two clearly had history, reconnecting like old friends. Archer was suddenly acutely aware of Sinclair watching her too closely. She felt herself tense, muscles tightening as her guard rose protectively.

Roberta made the introductions. "Archer, I'd like you to meet Dr. Vanessa Bonner. Dr. Bonner is the friend I was telling you about. I asked her to come so you could meet her, and maybe see if she'd be a good fit for you."

Dr. Bonner stepped forward. "It's very nice to meet you, Archer," she said as she extended a manicured hand.

Hesitating, Archer shot Sinclair a look. He gave her a nod and a smile meant to encourage her.

"Hi," she said, finally extending her own hand.

"I won't stay long," Dr. Bonner said, her too soft tone reminding Archer of the pink cotton candy she loved. "We thought this would be a good time for us to connect, maybe chat for a moment, and perhaps schedule something more formal at your convenience. If you feel comfortable with that, of course."

"Why don't you two make yourselves comfortable," Sinclair finally said, gesturing for them both to take a seat. "I promised Mom a walk in the woods so we're going to get out of your way. You're also welcome to use my office if you want more privacy."

"No, this is fine," Archer said, her voice quivering slightly.

Dr. Bonner smiled and nodded. "I think we'll be good."

Sinclair moved to Archer's side. He entwined his fingers with hers and leaned to kiss her cheek. His lips lingered there for a moment before he gave her hand one last squeeze. "It's okay," he whispered into her ear. "You won't have to do this alone. I'll be right here with you. For as long as you need me."

Archer took a deep breath and nodded, standing still as Sinclair and his mother, headed out the back door, closing it tightly behind them.

"So, how do we do this?" Archer asked. "How is this therapy going to work?" She and Dr. Bonner sat at the kitchen table facing each other.

"I'm here to help you navigate any issues that may be impacting your quality of life. The kind of treatment you receive will depend what we both feel will work best for your situation. I might ask you to tackle certain tasks designed to help you develop more effective coping skills. There may occasionally be homework assignments, like logging your reactions to particular situations as they occur. At some given time, you'll start to practice new skills between sessions. You might also have reading assignments so you can learn more about a particular topic. Like I said, it all depends on what we both decide you need that you're comfortable with doing."

"And exactly what kind of doctor are you?"

"I'm a licensed psychiatrist. I've gone to medical school and I have a Doctor of Medicine degree. If, at any time, we think medication may benefit you, unlike a psychotherapist, I can write you a prescription. I've also had extensive training in psychotherapy and psychoanalysis."

"Sounds like you've got all the bases covered."

Dr. Bonner smiled. "I think I'm well equipped to do my job and do it well, to be of great benefit to my patients."

"You come highly recommended so that counts for something." Archer smiled back.

"It's important that you feel comfortable with whomever you decide to work with. If, at any time, you don't feel we're meshing, I'll gladly refer you to someone else. It's going to take us both some time to learn to trust each other. Hopefully though, by the end of the first few sessions, you'll have a better understanding of your problem and I'll have given you a game plan to work through it."

"I have a crazy schedule and I have to travel a lot sometimes."

"That's fine. I completely understand your circumstances, so I can always come to you. My only request is that you commit fully to doing the work."

Archer met the woman's gaze. "So, when do I start?" she asked.

Dr. Bonner was gone by the time Sinclair and his mother made it back to the house. Roberta gave her son a quick glance as they stepped through the door.

"Are you hungry, son?"

He shook his head. "I could probably eat. I want to go check on Archer first though," he said as he peeked into the dining room and then the family room, not finding her in either spot.

His mother moved toward the kitchen. "She was exhausted. Check her room. I'm sure she's probably fast asleep."

With a nod of his head Sinclair turned and moved down the hall. Outside the bedroom door he knocked lightly. He was surprised when Archer answered, beckoning him inside. He pushed the door open and peered into the room.

Archer sat on the edge of the bed. She had showered, and changed, and was pulling a brush through the length of her hair. She waved him inside, a bright smile on her face.

"Come on in. How was your walk?"

"It was good. We went down to the pond and sat. It's one of my mother's favorite places to unwind. How did things go here for you?" Sinclair dropped down onto the bed beside her.

Archer nodded. "I made my first appointment. Dr. Bonner is coming back on Friday. I hope that's alright?"

Sinclair nodded. "That's fine. Whatever you need to do, Arch."

"I want to get one, maybe two sessions in before I leave for New York."

"New York?"

"I need to get into the studio. I have an album to make and I'm excited about it!"

Sinclair reached for her hand and squeezed it. "I'm excited for you, Arch!"

"Will you go with me?" she asked, shifting around to face him.

"To New York?"

"Roman says there's a production company there that you've worked with before. I thought maybe you could work on your film while I'm in the studio and when we're not working we can spend time together. There are still things I don't know about you. Things about each other that we both still have to learn. Getting my happy ending is going to require some effort from both of us."

He pondered her request for a moment, then nodded his head. "I need to maneuver some things around but I'm willing to make it happen if you are."

Archer jumped excitedly, tossing the hairbrush aside. She slid onto Sinclair's lap, wrapping her arms around his neck. Her eyes danced over his face. The look he was giving her was life-changing. It was as if he saw something in her she had yet to see in herself and she loved the glimmering reflection.

Sinclair exuded compassion and kindness and just being with him brought her comfort she had never fathomed. He was also too pretty for words, she thought as she traced the line of his profile with her eyes.

Hours later, Roberta knocked on the closed door. The dinner hour had come and gone, the food still sitting on the stovetop. She wasn't sure if she should be worried or not. When she got no answer, she pushed the structure open slowly, not wanting either of them to be surprised.

The couple lay fully clothed across the bed. Archer was curled in a fetal position with Sinclair wrapped warmly around her. Both were snoring, loud exhalations that echoed like small engines around the room. They were a sight to behold, resting peacefully together, looking like they'd always been meant for each other. Smiling, Roberta pulled the door closed and headed down the hallway back toward the kitchen.

TEN

"You really don't have to leave so soon," Sinclair said to his mother as she dropped her luggage at the front door. "You know you are always welcome to stay here for as long as you like."

"I have my own work to get back to," Roberta answered. "My agent rescheduled my last tour date, so I am headed to Italy. Your father is going to fly in for the concert and afterward we are going to spend some time on the Amalfi Coast. I am missing your old man and it is past time we spent some quality time together."

"I spoke to him earlier. He's a little miffed you didn't come home."

"I'll make it up too him. He understands I needed to check on you and your sister."

"She's miffed, too!"

Roberta laughed. "They'll both get over it." She reached up to kiss her son's cheek. "Take care of this one," she said as she gestured in Archer's direction. "I like her. She'll make me beautiful grandbabies!"

Archer laughed. She moved to hug the matriarch, the older woman wrapping her in a tight embrace. "Thank you for everything, Roberta," she said.

"If you need anything, you call me. Okay?"

Archer nodded. "I will. I promise. But I'm going to be okay."

Roberta smiled. "Baby girl, you're going to be *better* than okay!"

"You're still going to be able to do that thing with me, right?"

"I wouldn't pass up that opportunity for anything in this world!"

"What thing?" Sinclair questioned. He stepped in behind Archer, dropping his palms to her shoulders. "What are you two cooking up?"

Roberta eyed him with a raised brow and a wry smile. "Mind your own business, son! Let Archer and I mind ours."

Archer pressed her hand atop his, clutching his fingers warmly. She turned her head to give him a look, mischief dancing in her dark eyes.

Sinclair looked from one to the other and he laughed heartily. Together, they were going to be a force, he thought.

"That's my ride," Roberta said as the private car service taking her to the airport arrived. She threw open the front door just as the driver took the porch steps. "Good morning"," she said.

"Good morning, ma'am!" the man said. "Do you have any luggage?"

"I do," she said as she passed him her Samsonite carry-on bag and pointed toward her checked luggage.

The driver gathered her things and headed back to the trunk of his Town Car.

Roberta gave them both one last hug. "I'll call when I land. You two take care of each other, please!"

"Safe travels, Roberta!"

"Love you, Mom!"

As the car pulled out of the driveway, Sinclair and Archer waved until the vehicle was out of sight and Roberta was no longer waving back.

"So, what's on your agenda today?" Sinclair asked. He clasped his hand over Archer's and led her back into the house.

"Well, I thought we could pack up that leftover macaroni and cheese and that fried chicken your mother left in the refrigerator and maybe take a walk and have ourselves a picnic? I'd love to walk the property. I actually haven't seen much of the outside since I got here."

"That's actually a good idea. It'll give us a chance to relax."

"I'll go pack the food!"

"I'll pack the bug repellant and the bear spray."

"Bear...spray?"

Sinclair laughed. "We are in the forest. There are black bears. Coyotes, wolves, snakes, all kinds of wild animals."

Archer hesitated. "On second thought," she finally said, "scratch that. We'll picnic in the living room!"

The day had flown. Archer had arranged a blanket on the hardwood floor and they'd enjoyed lunch and then dinner there. Sinclair talked about his childhood, the good and the bad, sharing the moments that had molded him into a man he liked.

Archer had talked about her father, recalling the few memories she still had of him. There were moments when her eyes clouded with tears and others that had her laughing until she was doubled over clutching her sides.

Conversation between them was easy. They enjoyed talking to each other. It felt comfortable, and natural, and no topic was off limits. They talked politics, entertainment, and debated the merits of donuts with or without icing. At times, the conversation would be serious and intense and then just as easily would turn silly and casual. They were having a good time together and neither was ready for it to ever end.

"I can't believe it's after nine o'clock," Sinclair said. "I should probably go grab a shower and get to bed. I need to get some work done tomorrow. You do, too!" He leaned in to give her a kiss, his mouth gliding like silk against hers.

When they came up for air, Archer took a deep inhale of oxygen. She nodded her agreement. "It's actually been a long day," she said. "Why don't you go grab that shower and I'll straighten up here."

Sinclair kissed her one more time. "I can help."

She shook her head. "I got this. I need to call Roman before I head to bed anyway. I have five missed calls from him," she said as she stole a glance at her cell phone.

"Tell my brother-in-law I said hello, please."

"I will."

Sinclair squeezed her hand. "Good night, baby!"

"Sweet dreams, Sin!"

Sinclair stepped out of his shower and grabbed the large white towel he'd rested on the marble counter. He felt refreshed and energized, the feelings of sluggishness he'd felt just an hour earlier having dissipated.

He swiped the towel across his skin, drying the beads of moisture away. He was still thinking about Archer, unable to get the beautiful woman out of his head. There was no denying that Archer had become important to him. She consumed his thoughts, threads of her tying him into a knot when he least expected.

He trusted Archer and trust didn't come easily for him. Despite the obvious strides he had made in his relationship with his mother, he kept most people, women in particular, at arm's length. Most new relationships evolved slowly so it surprised him that his connection to Archer had happened so quickly. His mother had said he was in love. He hadn't denied it, but he hadn't been ready to embrace it either. In his small world, love had always been a dirty word. Ever since he'd been a little boy wanting his mother to love him and feeling like she didn't even like him.

What he was certain of though, was wanting Archer to be a permanent part of his life. She fueled his spirit and brought him joy he hadn't known before her. She made him laugh and with all the ugly he saw too often in the world, those moments of laughter were a priceless commodity.

He suddenly wondered what she was doing. Quietly hoping that she too had caught a second wind and might want to cuddle with him on the sofa, talking about everything and about nothing. He imagined holding her in his arms, the two of them making out like teenagers, and fantasized about feeling her up, his hands teasing her feminine spirit. He felt slightly foolish, and giddy with glee. Sinclair laughed out loud.

He wrapped the towel around his waist and stared into the mirror. His reflection was clouded, the residual steam hampering his view. He leaned closer to see, drawing his index finger over one eyebrow and then the other. After brushing his teeth, he debated whether to go to bed or search out Archer. A current of electricity shot through his groin, answering the confliction for him.

Sinclair moved from the bathroom to the bedroom. He came to an abrupt stop, finding Archer posed seductively atop his bed. His eyes widened in surprise.

She lay prone, her head propped against one hand, her mile-long legs crossed at the ankles. She was wearing lace. Black lace. A black lace bra and panty that accentuated every lush dip and curve of her body. Everything about her was sheer perfection and she took his breath away.

"Hi," she said softly, her lips bending upward in the sweetest smile.

His lips spread into a full grin, the wealth of it gleaning in his eyes. "Hi!"

"I thought we'd celebrate," Archer said. She lifted her torso, sitting upright as she pulled a knee to her chest, wrapping her arms around it.

"What are we celebrating?" he asked.

"My divorce. It's finally official. The judge signed on the dotted line today and I am now a free and single woman again."

"How do you feel about that?"

"Like a heavy weight has been lifted off my heart. Like I can start over again. Like I'm scared to death to take the next step." Her voice dropped to a loud whisper as she met his stare.

Sinclair was still standing in the middle of the room, frozen in place. He wanted to move but his legs were locked. His heartbeat was racing, and a raging erection had risen to attention. It was full and abundant, the protrusion tenting the front of that towel around his waist.

His gaze swept the length of her body, racing back and forth. He couldn't take his eyes off her. Her perky breasts filled the cups of her bra top, standing high beneath her top. The line of her lace bikini bottoms curved over her buttocks, exposing firm, ripe melons. Her voluptuous ass was perfectly round and intensely delectable. Sinclair suddenly realized he was salivating and he swallowed. He licked his lips, the gesture slow and methodic. There was no denying the desire that billowed between them.

"So," Archer said, a smile in her voice, "are you going to join me, Sin? Or do you plan to leave a girl hanging?" She crooked her finger, drawing him forward.

"Don't tease me, Arch. If we do this..." He paused, the thoughts in his head stalling.

Archer rose up on her knees, one hand pressed against her abdomen, the other reaching up to release her ponytail from the elastic band that held it at the nape of her neck. She shook her head, her hair falling down to her shoulders and framing her face. "I don't tease...much," she replied. "So, come here, Sin!" She bit down against her bottom lip, her eyes narrowing slightly.

Sinclair took three steps toward her. As he moved forward he let the towel fall to the floor, exposing every inch of his wanting. Archer gasped, loudly, the sight of Sinclair moving her to pant ever so slightly. Both could feel an electrifying energy pulling them to each other, a magnetic force neither could resist a moment longer.

Archer lifted her eyes to meet his stare as he made it to the edge of the bed and moved himself against her. She lifted her face to his and he gently kissed her mouth, savoring the softness of her lips. They were soon locked in a passionate embrace.

Archer responded by opening her mouth to Sinclair's invading tongue as it pushed past the line of her teeth and danced inside her mouth. The passion and energy were intoxicating. Sinclair was swallowing and licking her lips, savoring the taste of her. It was as if he'd been starved for her, an obsession finally fulfilled.

She felt his large hand pressing against the curve of her breast. Her nipples had hardened, rock hard protrusions begging for his attention. The friction of the lace fabric and the heat from his palm as he slowly kneaded her flesh had her temperature rising with a vengeance.

Sinclair slipped his hand between the lace and her skin. He pinched one nipple and then the other, then he cupped her beautiful breasts with both palms. He eased her down against the mattress, shifting himself above her.

Archer's entire body was throbbing, her most private place beating like a drumline gone awry. Her juices were beginning to puddle between her legs, feminine nectar flowing uncontrollably. She was wet and when he suddenly slid his fingers past the elastic of her panties, touching her sweet spot, she arched her back, curving herself against him in the sweetest ecstasy.

Sinclair's lips moved from her mouth, kissing along her profile to her neck, down to her clavicle and chest. His tongue followed where his hands led, kissing the round of her breasts and dipping into the valley of her cleavage.

He eased her bra straps off her shoulders, reaching around to unsnap it and slide it from her body. He threw the garment to the floor. Archer clutched the back of his head, encouraging his ministrations.

Theirs was suddenly a frantic display of desperate sexual ardor. Need like nothing either had ever known before. Her legs spread open as he slid her panties over her hips. She was freshly shaven and her feminine box was swollen with desire. His touch was teasing, igniting a wave of heat deep in her core that had her perspiring with anticipation.

With strength she wasn't expecting Sinclair snatched her hips up, pulling her legs over his shoulders and around his neck. Her buttocks were pressed to his chest as sat back on his haunches and pressed his face into her sweet spot. She screamed his name, murmuring a litany of decadent prayer over and over again.

He licked and sucked, savoring the sweet, flowing nectar, his tongue lashing at her softness. He suddenly glided his mouth from her crack to her clit and back, one flowing motion that had her begging for release. Archer was moaning and shaking, every nerve ending exploding like fireworks on the fourth of July.

Sinclair finally eased her back to the bed, shielding her body with his own. He eased himself into her, one swift push of his hips nestling him deep in the hot cavity. He hesitated as he savored the sensation of her inner lining welcoming him, her muscles clenching him tightly as her heat pulsed over his male member.

Lost in the emotions sweeping over them, Archer had no idea when he'd found a condom to sheath himself with and she didn't much care. She only knew that no other man would ever again know her this way. She was his, completely, heart, soul, and body and there would be no turning back. Sinclair was hers and she promised him, and God, she would never let him go.

She bit down against his shoulder, her nails raking the length of his back as he moved himself in and out of her, round and round, over and over, back and forth. They were both drunk with desire, the intensity of it echoing in the loud moans and grunts vibrating against the bedroom walls.

Her orgasm hit like a monsoon, the intensity of it inciting his. He screamed his pleasure into her mouth as he captured her lips and kissed her fervently. Her legs were wrapped around his waist and she tightened the hold she had on him as she met his strokes with her own. With one final plunge they fell off the edge of ecstasy together, the moment sealing their fates forever.

EPILOGUE

The red-carpet event for the Sinclair Cooper documentary, *Arch*, was a star-studded gala of industry elites in film and music. Cameras flashed and paparazzi called for their attention as Archer and Sinclair stepped out of the black limousine.

Archer looked spectacular in a Giorgio Armani evening gown that had been designed especially for her. The one-shouldered gown was pleated across the bust and cascaded down to an organza and sequined skirt with an extended train. The copper-colored fabric complemented her dark complexion and would grace the cover of every fashion magazine the following morning.

Sinclair wore a tailored Armani tuxedo, the classic styling complementing his good looks. Side they side they were too beautiful for words. The couple posed for photographs before being led into the theater for the film's screening.

The stunning couple had been the talk of the town since the unexpected release of Archer's platinum-selling album, *My Sin*. A departure from her usual chart-topping pop songs, her newest catalogue of music was a testament to the depth of her talent. Critics and fans had been in awe of the soulful, bluesy, gut-wrenching music that had garnered her Grammy nominations for Album of the Year, Song of the Year, and Record of the Year. She'd led the musical rat pack with twelve nominations total and was predicted to run away with each one. Sinclair couldn't have been prouder.

Roberta Cooper met them in the lobby, wringing her hands together nervously. She smiled when she saw them, relief washing over her face. "Finally! I was starting to think you two weren't going to make it!"

"It's all Sin's fault," Archer said as she tossed her husband a look. A coy smile blessed her expression.

Sinclair shrugged his broad shoulders. "You want grandchildren!" he said, his eyebrows raised suggestively. "That requires..."

His mother shook her head, holding up her hand to stall his comment. "No need to explain! In fact, that is more information than I needed."

The family all laughed as the matriarch hugged them both.

Roman suddenly came rushing across the room. "Did you two lose your phones? I've been calling you both for the last hour!"

"It's all Sin's fault," Archer said again. She laughed heartily.

Sinclair grinned. "How's it going?

Roman shook her head. "The film's almost over and the movie critics have already started posting their reviews. It's definitely a hit. One critic said he wouldn't be surprised if this is your year for an Emmy. Congratulations!" He slapped Sinclair warmly against the back.

Archer leaned up to kiss Sinclair's lips. "This is our year, Mr. Cooper."

"Yes, it is, Mrs. Cooper," he said as he kissed her back.

"Are you two ever going to announce your marriage to the public?" Roman asked. "I've already prepared a statement. Just in case you might want to make a statement tonight?"

Sinclair shrugged his shoulders. "My wife says our personal life is off-limits, and so it will be. We have no comment."

Archer rolled her eyes skyward. "I don't even need to answer that question. You will not get me worked up before I have to perform."

"Speaking of," Roman said as he took a glance at his wrist watch. "The film should wrap in about ten minutes. Then I will introduce you both. Sinclair, you will give your filmmaker speech, say whatever you want about making the documentary, maybe share a tidbit or two about the star. Then you'll introduce Archer, and your mother, and they'll perform. After that, there will be a brief Q&A with the press. Any questions?"

Everyone shook their heads, gazes sweeping between them.

"I think we're all good, Roman," Archer said. She gave her mother-in-law a smile. "I'm excited. I hope you are!"

Roberta nodded. "I am, and I'm honored that you wanted me to do this song with you tonight."

"He's your Sin, too. I couldn't do it without you," Archer said, referring to her album's title track, *My Sin*. The song was currently sitting in the number one spot on the Billboard charts and the ode to her love for Sinclair was her favorite.

Sinclair grinned. They'd all come a long way since that first meeting on the Grammy red carpet. He and Archer had both grown exponentially. He couldn't begin to measure the joy she'd brought to his life.

The two women turned, Roman leading the way toward the stage. Sinclair called her name.

"Arch!"

Archer turned, her gaze locking with his. "Yes, Sin?"

"I love you," he said, the words echoing around the room.

Archer grinned. "I love you, too!"

ABOUT THE AUTHOR

Writing since she was old enough to put pen to paper, Deborah Fletcher Mello firmly believes that for her, writing is as necessary as breathing. Her first novel, TAKE ME TO HEART, earned her a 2004 Romance Slam Jam nomination for Best New Author. In 2008, Deborah won the Romantic Times Reviewers Choice award for Best Series Romance for her ninth novel, TAME A WILD STALLION. Her publication, CRAVING TEMPTATION was named one of Publisher's Weekly Best Books for 2014 and was also nominated for a 2015 Emma Award for Book of the Year. As well, her novel PLAYING FOR KEEPS was a Library Journal Best of 2015 and won the Romantic Times Reviewer's Choice award for Best Multicultural Romance. Deborah was named the 2016 Romance Slam Jam Author of the Year and most recently, was honored to be named BRAB's Reading Warriors Choice 2017 Breakout Author. Born and raised in Fairfield Country, Connecticut, Deborah maintains base camp in North Carolina but considers home to be wherever the moment moves her.

Made in the USA
Lexington, KY
20 February 2018